THE YARASTAR TRILOGY

BOOK ONE

The Unmarked Girl

JEANELLE FRONTIN

mark made

GROUP LTD.

Book Cover & Character Illustration by Israel Silva

Author photograph by Damian Luk Pat

Publication Data
Frontin, Jeanelle.
The Unmarked Girl / Jeanelle Frontin.
ISBN pb: 978-976-8255-76-1
ISBN ebook: 978-976-8255-77-8

First Edition

mark made
GROUP LTD.

DEDICATION

To Alyxander, my son:

You taught me the true meaning of being a vessel when I was blessed with carrying you within me. After birthing the greatness that is you, I've always known I could do anything I ever wanted.

With this freedom of heart, mind, and soul, after a labor of profound ferocity, I've pushed out this baby dream: The Unmarked Girl.

In another world, like Mira, Yara is your older sister and friend… I hope she will always remind you, in the face of the unfathomable, where your purest power lies.

~

Chapter One

She was in the dark place again. They all ran up to her. Pointing. Taunting. Loathing...

"What is she?!"

"Where did they find her?"

"Why did they bring her here?"

"She is not even one of us!"

"Why does she look like that?"

"Where are her markings?"

"What are you?"

"Are you a Skotad?"

"Is she a weapon?"

"WHERE DID YOU COME FROM?"

"WHAT ARE YOU?"

"WHO ARE YOU?!"

Yara's body jolted as her eyes flew open. Shivers ran through her at the sound of the strange, soft voice. She felt cold even though she was swaddled in the furs from the feathered trees. Her brows furrowed around her eyes' iridescent irises as she lay in her room in the dwelling.

Yara had grown quite used to the disparaging noise of her Tribe's voices in her sleep. This voice had been a recent addition. Still, it wasn't the perplexity of its sudden presence that shook her. It was the eerie, ethereal language in which it spoke—a language she certainly did not know. Yet somehow, from a place deep below the chaos of the dream, she understood its meaning:

"YaraStar... do you know who you are?"

No... I don't, she thought bitterly.

Yara rubbed her eyes and glanced around her wooden room. It had been carved out from a giant Saptree by her own Tribe father. Its walls and ceiling were covered in markings. It was said that they told of ancient stories and of times to come. These markings were found naturally on the trunk of every Saptree, and on all living things on Mira. They were sacred. They were the markings made by Sunstar on all that was special.

"But I, the UNMARKED, am not," she muttered, quickly lowering her voice as she heard her parents tinkering around their dwelling. She would never want them to be concerned or think she was ungrateful. She knew she was, at least, very special to them. It humbled her every day.

Her thoughts drifted back to the day she had asked her parents why she seemed to be the only unmarked living thing on Mira. It often bothered her, even more than her odd blue hair and weirdly colored eyes. Lana and Sorin never knew what to say in those moments. No one knew where Yara had come from, for without markings, there was no traceable birthline. Still, Lana would try to remind her that even though she found her as an unmarked baby, she knew Yara was a gift from Sunstar.

Yara felt the opposite. Markings were a sign of origin in Photaks, and even in Skotads. They traced back their generations and heritage, and also their skills. Each person was born with them prominently displayed all over their bodies. Everyone knew their birthline. As a result, everyone knew their natural talents although there were no restrictions on what you could become. The warriors, the food-gatherers, the Elders and the Chief, the teachers, the makers, and even the musicians were all marked.

The Tribe had never been accepting of what they saw as an unmarked abomination. When the Elders' vote had allowed Yara to remain, the village became tense with fear and displeasure. Many stood against it, but the vote's resolution could not be changed.

Almost sixteen years had passed since Lana had found Yara, and while much of the villagers' coldness remained, so much more had changed. Yara was training to be a warrior for her Tribe, and she was incredibly skilled at it. All the other trainees in her year begrudgingly admired her strength, speed, and bravery. Yara knew she needed to work hard to prove herself, so she always ensured she was ahead of all the other trainees. It hadn't taken her long to leave them all behind… all, in fact, except for Kristos.

The smile that crept over Yara's face at the thought of Chief Lamad's only son was not a reaction of which she was often very conscious. As she stretched her long, lean body into the softness of her swaddling, she felt the familiar tinge of excitement. She shook off the aftereffects of the eerie voice in her dream and willed herself to focus. She may not know who she was or where she had come from, but Yara knew what she was going to become… who she needed to become. A Photak warrior.

She rushed to get ready to meet Kristos, strapping on her trainee garb as quickly as her fingers would allow. She went out into the living area of her dwelling. It was a warm, wooden room that kept many of her best memories in its carved walls. She chattered about her final training days to Sorin while he ate and while Lana placed food in her mouth between sentences.

In less than a week, at the age of sixteen, both Kristos and Yara were to be inducted as true Photak warriors. Yara was the only other person in the Tribe who could match his combat level. As a result, they were paired since they initiated, each at the age of eight. Yara was a solid practice partner for Kristos, and they trained together almost every day.

Kissing both of her Tribe parents goodbye, she walked out into the dewy, delicate warmth of the new day. It was always bright as there had been no night for thousands of years. The habitable side of Mira had faced Sunstar since its core was damaged. While the planet no longer rotated, Sunstar still did. It allowed for subtle hints of time and the marking of days. Mornings had always been Yara's favorite time of day. Mornings were also the time that Yara and Kristos trained.

As Yara strode along the winding path, she breathed in the fresh air deeply. Her subconscious smile appeared again, along with its usual rush of energy. She would never openly admit it, but seeing Kristos did that to her. Yara had a hard time dealing with her most naked feelings. She dressed them up in layers of stoic seriousness to a fault. While she felt certain at times that some of the chemistry she felt for Kristos was returned, he had always just been respectful and caring. Still, she enjoyed being the only one he was close to in the village, much to the jealous confusion of the other Photak girls. Shortly after being inducted as a warrior, he would have to choose a mate, and Yara couldn't help but wonder if a part of her was more excited about the possibility...

No, she thought with surety, *nothing compares to finally becoming a warrior.*

Yara walked past the village dwellings towards the path to the Soar. It was the secret place that she and Kristos met to train since he stumbled upon her there a decade ago. He had found Yara feverishly attacking a feathered tree when she was just six years old. Kristos had instinctively known why. A Skotad had dangerously attacked her mother while she was gathering food in the Greens. He saw the fire it placed within Yara and felt her pain. With her permission, he began training with her that very day.

Kristos had always been kind to Yara. He never seemed to be troubled by her strange appearance. In fact, he found her looks to be nothing short of fascinating, and her battle skills even more so. He commented openly on them both all the time. Over the years, he had become Yara's only true friend.

Kristos and Yara were also the two best warrior trainees the Tribe had ever seen. They honed their combat techniques with such acclaimed precision, speed, and strength that some of the village's children could at times be seen in mock battles donning blue scarfs on their heads.

"YaraStar! YaraStar!"

The delighted shouts of Yara's biggest little fan interrupted her nostalgic thoughts. Mila flung herself into the air and straight into Yara's outstretched arms.

"Yara, Mother took my blue scarf," Mila complained, "but she doesn't know I found out where she hid it!"

Giggling mischievously, Mila pried open her pocket to reveal a dirty, balled-up blue rag.

"Aww, Mi—"

"MILA!"

Both Yara and Mila swung around to see Mila's mother, May, whose face seemed to be filling with increasing rage at the sight of Mila in Yara's arms. In a flash, Mila slid down and disappeared into the bushes while May shouted after her. May glared at Yara then stomped off after Mila.

"Blue-haired nuisance," May muttered loud enough for Yara to hear as she disappeared behind the shrubs.

Yara sighed. She loved the children in the village. They never treated her like a strange-looking outsider. In fact, she felt most comfortable around them, and especially around Mila. The Tribe's children saw her as the strong warrior she knew she was, and they loved her for it. She could never understand why their parents didn't encourage such open-mindedness in them. She bitterly vented it to Kristos upon arriving at the Soar.

Kristos usually didn't say much during times like these. As he tilted his head listening, his brilliantly red hair fell to one side of his face. His brown eyes echoed with a sense of sadness, wanting to comfort her despair. However, he seemed to understand that she just needed to speak her mind and let it out. She didn't want to be pitied.

Instead, on days like today, Yara would want to fight hard. She would give more than her all into the day's training. Becoming a Photak warrior meant becoming fully accepted, or at least as close to acceptance as she could get. More than that, it would mean everyone, including Mila's mother, would respect her. It was, after all, Photak tradition.

Yara lowered herself into her original,

signature stance, with one outstretched arm curved towards Sunstar and the other stretched towards Kristos.

"Let's begin," she said.

Kristos responded quickly, leaping towards her with his gold-tanned, mountainous form. Yara twisted gracefully out of his way, propelling and landing her leg into his back before he could even touch the ground. Kristos flipped as he hit the ground, pushing off almost as quickly as he touched it and flying towards her. He lunged into her, grabbing her in his arms, but then within a second, she was loose and spiraling again.

Yara had created an unusual combat style that was notoriously difficult to predict. The offbeat moves came with their own rhythm, and from an outsider's perspective, it looked like a dangerous, deadly dance. Kristos, as the son of the Chief, was an expert in the traditional Photak fighting style and had already created new moves for the Tribe. While

Yara regularly practiced those Photak methods when around others, and was extremely capable in them, she kept her signature style for her private training sessions with Kristos.

For hours, they plunged deeper and deeper into the forms and fundamentals of their weaponized bodies, each tranced by the other's savage drive for utter perfection. A routine practice was never complete until every move and countermove was mastered, and a session was never over until each person had attained mastery. They were both far more advanced than what was even needed to be inducted as a warrior. They were only held back from joining the official ranks by the mandatory requirement of eight consecutive years of training.

When they finally finished, Yara and Kristos perched upon their usual boulder in the Soar, drinking their sapjuice for recovery.

"Can you imagine what it would be like...?" Yara said softly. Her eyes were fixed upon the border of the Greens as the rays of Sunstar melted into her olive skin.

The Soar was dangerously close to the Greens, and Tribe members who weren't warriors or gatherers were warned away from being close enough for a brazen Skotad to grab or attack them. It was precisely for that reason both Yara and Kristos had chosen that location, knowing they would generally be undisturbed. Except, of course, when Mila would sneak there with her little friends to observe new fight moves.

"I think I've trained every day of my life for this," Yara continued, "and just knowing I will be able to protect the Tribe and even avenge my mother..."

Kristos nodded silently. They sat quietly for some time before he turned to her with a serious look on his face.

"Yara..." he hesitated, then continued, "I have never wanted to pry... but have you ever wondered about your birth parents? Who they really are?"

"Yeah. Sure. And they must be hideous by the looks of me!" she disparagingly remarked with a laugh. She hated it when his questions got this serious. She already had to deal with her incessant thoughts by day and torturous dreams by night.

And now that weird, eerie voice, she thought, remembering how different her dreams had become of late.

His reaction to her answer, however, was one of anger—a rare side she saw only when she pushed things too far.

"Why do you say these awful things about yourself?" he demanded. "Yara, you're the most beautiful girl I've ever seen!"

Yara stared at him, speechless. Most of the times, he would roll his eyes in annoyance and curse under his breath. There was even one time that he had walked off and left her alone in the Soar.

While she was used to him building her confidence by saying kind things to her, he had never made such a bold statement, especially in comparison to anyone else. Yara stared at the ground and shifted uncomfortably.

This time, Kristos sighed. It was his way of saying he knew he had pushed it too far as well.

"Look, I know it has been hard for you. No one denies that this Tribe has made it hard for you and your Tribe parents. But I am in line to be the next Chief, and I just wanted you to know... if you ever want to search for them, we can... and we will. You're a Photak, Yara. A Photak warrior. And if you want to find them," he said softly, "then this is my promise to you, YaraStar. We will."

***

Her walk home felt like a trance. Yara didn't even notice the usual glares of annoyance from some passing villagers. She didn't even hear the mutterings under their breath.

He called me a Photak, she thought, *a Photak warrior.*

She could not think of a moment in her life that meant more to her than that one. There was nothing she had ever wanted more than this. To belong, to be a real part of the Tribe, to fight alongside them without being seen as an outsider. To be joined to her mate…

No, he isn't mine, she thought, immediately correcting herself.

However, her feelings about his words were nothing less than hopeful. She had a chance. A real chance. The Chief's only son said those words, and for the first time, she felt that perhaps she did have a place here.

As she walked into her dwelling, Yara hugged her father tightly and then twirled around her mother.

"Well, I know you enjoy training," her father said raising his eyebrow, "but I haven't seen you smile this way since we surprised you with sensopa on your twelfth birthday!"

Sensopa was a sweet, crusted pie made from the most precious ingredients found in the Greens. It was rare for a family of her parents' markings to be able to afford one, but that year had been a good one.

"Well..." Yara started, barely containing her blush, "today, after training, Kristos called me a real Photak. A Photak warrior!"

She decided to exclude the part about finding her birth parents as she didn't want her Tribe parents to feel like she saw them as inadequate in any way. They were, after all, quite the opposite.

"Can you imagine?!" Yara squealed as she continued, "He sees ME that way. And the look in his eyes..."

Yara hugged both her parents while spinning gracefully and then made her way to soak off the day. She didn't see the worried look her parents gave each other as she walked away.

Chapter Two

Three days before the Calling, the official day when the trainees would be inducted as Photak warriors, the aspiring warriors were to meet with the Elders and Chief Lamad for their final lessons. These lessons served to reinforce the history of the Tribe and the seriousness of the commitment before them. Photak warriors were required on the Day of the Calling to dedicate their lives to the protection of the Tribe against the Skotads and to give their lives without hesitation. It was the most honorable tribute a Photak could make. The privileges granted to warriors were elevated as a sign of respect for risking their lives to ensure the protection of all.

When Yara first learned of this, she was already a few years into her training, and she felt even more motivated to succeed. Photak warriors were seen as equals, regardless of the markings of their lines and their families' origins. They were just under the ranking of the Chief and Elders. Yara would be the first warrior of both of her Tribe parents' lineages, and she felt extremely proud to raise the quality of their livelihood for the rest of their lives. Her parents had been partially shunned because of their decision to keep her, so it was her way of giving them even more than what they had lost.

Equals, she thought, as she made her way to the training grounds for the lessons. She felt comfort wash over her. It had been difficult being an outcast, and even more difficult not knowing why she was born this way. Yara wished the Photaks could simply accept that her physical appearance meant nothing. She could dance in the rays of Sunstar just like any other Photak, something a Skotad could never do. To her, it was the only determining factor that mattered as it proved she was not a Skotad, even more than not having the Skotads' silver-white hair and pale-skinned features. She may not have markings and the Photaks' red hair, but she felt within herself that she was definitely a Photak.

Just an ugly Photak with defects that caused my cowardly parents to discard me as a baby in the Greens, she thought bitterly.

Over the years, she had tried not to think about her possible origins and horrific birth parents. It filled her with too much rage. She didn't care who they were or where they were from. She just wanted to know why they couldn't love her in the way her Tribe parents did. Her Tribe parents had been willing to risk their lives and future to keep her because they loved her at first sight, no matter how she looked.

As she entered the training grounds, she looked around her at the beauty of the rich flora and took a deep breath. Feathered trees surrounded the boulders that encrusted red glass shards, a material that the Photaks often fashioned for weapons. Mira was a beautiful planet, at least on the side that faced Sunstar. Not many had ever journeyed to Mira's dark side as nothing grew there. Thus, neither Photak nor Skotad could survive. There were rumors of majestic structures left in ruins from the Great War of the Planets, but many millennia had passed since then.

Yara walked past the Elders, nodding respectfully, and headed towards the main keep where the warriors-in-training had gathered. The other trainees gave her labored looks of acknowledgment, and a little way off, Chief Lamad smiled as he chatted with Pekone, the Photak weapons' creator and head instructor.

Yara couldn't wait to finally be allowed to step foot into the shadowed Greens, and to see and fight a Skotad, both for the first time. Despite this, she couldn't deny the value of the years of instruction that preceded warrior induction. In that period, she had also grown particularly fond of Pekone. He was a gruff old man with a long fiery beard. He didn't seem to like anyone, and it made her feel that he saw her just like he saw anyone else. While he wasn't an Elder, he was still seen as a mentor to all warriors and was one of the most respected Photaks in the Tribe.

Pekone had the combined markings of a warrior and a creator, making his bloodline the only ones gifted in the art of light-wielding for weaponry. He had recently upgraded the Guiding Threads. They were unbreakable strings with a light aura that helped new warriors find their way in and out of the shadowed Greens until their eyes adjusted to the Blurry.

The Blurry was the word Photaks used to describe their inability to see clearly in shadows and darkness. If they stayed too long in the Blurry, the consequences would be devastating. Some Photaks, according to their birthline, were naturally better than others in adjusting their eyes in and out of the shadowy Greens. Among all Photaks, Pekone's tribal line was the most adept.

As Yara found a place to settle for the day, she thought about what it would be like to have a real tribal line. She threw her things down to the ground in annoyance at herself. She usually tried to ignore those types of thoughts, but today she felt a bit on edge. She felt even more annoyed as she turned to see Kristos arriving, greeting his father and Pekone.

"Stupid Kristos!" she muttered to herself.

She realized his questioning a few days ago

had probably been the reason her origins were on her mind. Kristos turned and smiled brightly when he saw her. She forced a happy smile and waved in return as she sat to adjust her trainee garb. As she saw him leave his father and come towards her, she mentally reprimanded herself for even allowing the topic to fester.

A soft wind began to blow, refreshingly cooling the training grounds. Then, suddenly, it was there with her. Right beneath the gentle breeze that brushed her blue locks off her face. Softly. But right… there.

"YaraStar… do you know who you are?"

Yara jolted uncontrollably by the eerie whisper and its unknown tongue just as Kristos jogged up to meet her. Her face lost all color, and her body involuntarily trembled. That voice belonged in her dream world, not here. She felt like she must be losing her mind.

"Yara, are you okay?" Kristos stooped down, concern rippling from his deep-brown eyes into hers.

"Yes..." she said uncomfortably, "I just thought I heard... it's nothing."

Yara mentally scolded herself, and forced another smile to her face. She gave Kristos a quick shove.

"The inner fight is at the end of today, you know," she said smugly. "And the Elders and the Chief will witness it. I'm going to be chosen as the one who defends the Photak Tribe."

Kristos laughed heartily at her enthusiasm though his face still showed echoes of concern. He knew she was changing the topic, but he didn't want to force anything out of her. Yara was generally private, and she was way too much of a rebel. Insistent prying was always met with strong resistance.

"You don't know that you'll be chosen yet!"

he teased. "And because I am the Chief's son, it can't be me! You're still in second place, Yara, and if you're giving too much trouble, they'll send me in after you!"

Yara felt a surge of hope sweep over her. The warrior-in-training who won the inner fight would be seen as having answered the Call and would become the first inducted warrior. Given all she had been through to finally reach this day, there was nothing she desired more.

Before the inner fight could take place, the Photak lessons would be imparted. In them, the history of the Tribes and of Mira, their unmoving planet, would be recounted. It was crucial that the Photak warriors knew why they fought and what was at stake, so that in the darkest of times they could anchor to the power of that truth.

The trainees and warriors all took their place upon the boulders and looked towards the elevated stone structure. Chief Lamad took his place at the head of the stones with the Elders surrounding him equally, four on either side. As the Elders solemnly sat in unison, Chief Lamad's lessons began:

"Thousands of years have passed since our Mira's rotations were halted. We were attacked by a powerful weapon of a people from a shadow planet beyond our own. Their weapon targeted the deepwater core of Mira where all its power and lifeforce resided. It was meant to annihilate all who dwelled on our planet, and to completely destroy it. It is said that with its final amount of lifeforce, Sunstar allowed the core to send out a pulse to all living things upon the surface. It was just enough to allow us to continue to live but not for Mira to keep rotating. We were left only with the guidance of the sacred symbols. These markings connect us to Mira's spirit and Sunstar's will. They tell the stories of our past, to keep our birthlines alive, and to chart the way to our future without the core. These sacred markings are Sunstar's blessings to all living things... even to the evil Skotads."

Yara shifted uncomfortably as some of the trainees sent smug looks in her direction. A few of the Elders glanced coldly toward where she sat. She heard Kristos whisper a few reassuring words, but it didn't change how she felt. Now more than ever, her perfectly clear skin stood out. Only when the Chief looked over and gave her a small, almost apologetic, smile did she feel herself breathe again. He continued his lesson.

"There was once a time before the planet's attack when there were both days and nights. Skotads have never been blessed to be able to withstand the rays of our Sunstar, so they stayed in their mountains and tunnels during the day. Still, they had no reason back then to fear Sunstar as they could roam unrestricted and gather food at night.

"The evil Skotads knew that at night the Photaks' vision would be blurry at best. They would wreak havoc on our villages, killing many and taking our Photak children into their mountain caves and tunnels, never to be seen again. Our warriors they would keep for three days before releasing them, as the Skotads knew the grave repercussions of not staying in Sunstar's light. The warriors' blurry eyesight would become as clear as a Skotad's to enable sight in their darkness. However, the consequence of this was irreversible: for now, in Sunstar's light, the Photaks' ability to see would be gone. Their eyesight would degrade to complete Light Blindness. When our warriors were released, this Light Blindness would cause unstoppable, incurable pain upon exposure to Sunstar. Such a Blinded Photak would essentially become akin to a Skotad and would never be able to live in the rays of Sunstar again."

Although she already knew the danger of the Greens, Yara shuddered at the thought of being unable to see or dwell in the warming rays of Sunstar. What scared her was not just how much she loved the light, but that it was her only connection to the Photak Tribe. Her ability to dwell in the rays of Sunstar had been the reason her mother was able to carry her to the village after she found her in the Greens. It was also the only reason the Elders had even considered allowing her to stay.

The Chief's voice grew dark.

"Sunstar grew angry. The Skotads did not respect us as the light dwellers. Their jealousy of Sunstar's blessings upon the Photaks resulted in nothing short of hateful, gruesome acts of increasing violence. While we will always mourn the damage to our Mira's core, we know that Sunstar allowed the shadow planet to win. Sunstar did this so that there would be an end to the Skotad violence.

"With Mira no longer rotating on its axis, only one side of the planet has faced Sunstar's rays ever since. As all living things need the light of Sunstar to survive, the dark side of our planet became a barren wasteland. Many of the Skotads died of starvation because they could no longer leave their tunnels to gather food in the now ever-present light. We know this was Sunstar's wrath against the Skotads, for there was only day and no more night."

As the Chief drew near to the end of his lesson of truth, the warriors present shouted occasional war cries in support.

"Then the greenery that was once in balance with nature became thick and overgrown from Sunstar's continuous energy. Soon, the shadowed Greens crept up upon the hills, to the mountains and their tunnels. The last few surviving Skotads were finally able to sustain themselves by going into the dark Greens. They began to build back their numbers as the centuries passed. While it was thought then that maybe they had learned their lesson and would finally acknowledge the Photaks as Sunstar's chosen people, they instead decided to retaliate. Now... the never-ending war continues.

"Warriors-in-training, this is not just their

fight against you… it is their defiance of Sunstar's clear instruction and blessing upon the Photaks. When you are sent into the Greens to protect our people and our village, you will also be defending the will of Sunstar. Every fight you win, every Skotad you defeat… it is the highest honor that you can show to Sunstar, and to us as your leaders. Because we… WE, the chosen, are the ones who walk in light!"

"WE, THE CHOSEN, ARE THE ONES WHO WALK IN LIGHT!"

All those present, including Yara, repeated the Tribal words in fierce solidarity. She may have heard versions of this lesson of Truth before, but today, it meant so much more to her. It was the one thing no one could take away from her—she too was a chosen, enough to at least be able to walk in light. Perhaps, Sunstar would favor her desire to be a warrior and to dedicate her life to protecting the Photaks, finally granting her a place of belonging.

As each Elder said their words of wisdom to the trainees, the time drew closer for the inner fight defender to be announced. The Guiding Threads were finally being gifted to each of the trainees. This meant that the announcement of the defender would follow. One by one, the trainees went up to the Chief as he called their names. Pekone stood with the Chief, handing the Guiding Thread to each warrior-in-training personally and saying something quietly to each of them.

As Yara's name was called, she walked up somewhat awkwardly to the stones. The Chief gave her a soft smile, and then she faced Pekone with her arm outstretched. Pekone placed the Guiding Thread in her open hand and stared with deadly focus into Yara's iridescent eyes. Seconds passed, and Pekone said nothing. He also did not remove his hand from the instrument of light. Eventually, he spoke.

"For you... Yara..."

It was all he said. Then he released her hand and looked away. Yara walked back to the boulder she was sharing with Kristos.

"What did he tell you?" Kristos asked with humored intrigue. "I've never seen Pekone stare at someone like that before."

Yara quoted what he said, and Kristos' expression seemed to change from amused to confused. She immediately questioned him back, but he hesitated to answer. Yara insisted.

"He said, 'for you, chosen of Sunstar,'" Kristos said softly.

Yara turned away and gritted her teeth. She felt embarrassed, and a bit peeved. It was her first indication that Pekone didn't consider her to be like the rest of the warriors-in-training. She didn't like how it felt. The more she replayed it in her mind, the more the rage she had been trying to control surfaced into her consciousness.

Focus, Yara, don't spiral, she thought angrily.

It was already too late. She was angry. She had done so much to prove herself for years. She just needed one thing now… one thing to show them what she was really made of and to finally put an end to their doubts. She needed to be the chosen defender of the inner fight.

The Chief and Elders sat with Pekone and went into a hushed discussion on the stones. All the Guiding Threads had been issued so there could only be one thing left for that day. A few of the Elders glanced towards her.

Yara's heartstar leapt. She felt nervousness creep in, cooling the edge off of her rage. She found herself saying a subconscious prayer to Sunstar. If they chose her, it would mean that Sunstar had finally heard her prayers after sixteen years. In fact, it would be nothing short of a sign to her that she finally had a place in this world… perhaps even a sign that she was somewhat special to Sunstar.

The Chief stood up. It was time.

Chapter Three

"As you all know, the inner fight honors the warrior-in-training who has shown the most advancement over the past eight years. While Kristos has long been known to be that person, he, as my son, cannot take the place of the defender. The Elders and I have deliberated on this, and we have found that there is no trainee more deserving of this honor... than Yara..."

Yara could barely hear the gasps and loud,

grumbling objections of those present over the pounding of her heartstar. She sat frozen for a second, wondering if she was in a dream and sleeping back in her swaddling. It was Kristos' voice that brought her back to reality.

"Well done, Yara!" he exclaimed, grabbing her. "There is none more deserving than you, and I know that firsthand!"

Yara shot up and gave a quick, formal acknowledgment of her acceptance and sat back down, still in a haze. As Chief Lamad dismissed the trainees for a short recess, Yara wished her parents could be there to witness this. Only warriors were allowed in these final sessions, but she knew they would still get the news before it was even over. She could imagine the looks on their faces, a mixture of shock, awe, and pride with so much love. She sighed at the thought and turned to look at Kristos who still hadn't yet taken his eyes off of her. She appreciated his patience, sitting there with her, allowing her to take it all in. He seemed to always know when to leave her to her thoughts and when to speak.

"Does it feel like you thought it would?" he asked as her hazy expression melted into gleaming joy.

"It's better..." she whispered with an unusual amount of humility. "I can't believe it's even happening..."

"Modesty?" Kristos teased. "Another first already?"

Yara punched him in the arm and flashed him a sweet smile. She didn't even care to fire back with her usual feistiness. All she knew was that she felt something she was sure she had never felt before, and as the haze cleared, Yara instinctively knew what it was. It was happiness. Not happiness in spite of, or happiness for the sake of... just pure, true happiness.

Kristos stared at Yara with pride. He couldn't wait for everyone to see what she could really do.

Her deadly dance style that only he had seen was sure to impress even the most disagreeable Elder, perhaps even Elder Malek.

Pekone was responsible for umpiring the inner fight. Soon, he walked up to them and sat, giving a small, courteous smile with a hint of warmth. He held the Sleeper in his hand, and he studied it for a moment to ensure the dosage was correct. Yara would be drugged slightly with it. While the Sleeper was a weapon used to capture and interrogate Skotads, it was also used in the inner fight to weaken the defender. The intention was to mimic the strength level of a Photak who had been almost three days in the Greens. Under the Sleeper, the inner fight challenge would be to fight off a select group of warriors-in-training one by one, so that the fight could simulate escaping the Greens against all the odds.

"The Sleeper is designed and dosed to make you weak, but you won't be knocked out," Pekone explained, "and I should tell you… there is an elusive component in it that will make everything feel much worse."

Pekone paused and seemed to be taking his time to find the right words to explain and instruct.

"Try to anchor to something within you, like a memory or a moment that you know is real and meaningful. When things feel a bit crazy, it is your only way back to reality and back to the fight. Do everything in your power to concentrate on the trainees being sent in to attack you. I know you have trained for many things, but you have never fought under these circumstances. The Sleeper gets stronger before it subsides, so whatever you feel at first will only get worse. Remember, if you win, you will be the first named at the Calling, and your place as a warrior will be secure. But if you lose, it does not mean you won't still be Called… You will instead have to be considered by the Chief and Elders alongside all your peers… So just do your very best."

Pekone put his hand out, and Yara placed her arm gently into it.

"This inner fight is for you, Yara. Are you ready?" he asked.

Yara nodded confidently.

"Don't forget: choose your memory, your anchor, now. Once I inject you with the Sleeper, there is no turning back."

"I've already chosen..." she said, and unconsciously glanced towards Kristos with a small smile.

Kristos grinned, making Yara aware of what she might have heedlessly revealed. As she groaned slightly, Pekone grunted in response and firmly sunk the Sleeper into her arm.

Everything in Yara's world began to spin.

"Anchor, Yara, anchor!" she heard Pekone order.

Kristos called me a real Photak warrior, she

thought to herself.

The world stilled, and while still weak, Yara stood up strong. Pekone looked towards Chief Lamad and nodded.

"LET THE INNER FIGHT BEGIN!" Lamad shouted to the sound of the warriors' war cries.

Yara walked towards the red circle that was drawn in the center of the grounds. The warriors and trainees parted to let her through, and some shot disapproving looks in her direction. Kristos followed right behind her as a show of his support.

Yara's steps felt light and a bit unstable, but she found the sensation tolerable. She wondered what her fighting spins would feel like in such a lightheaded state. She thought that the four rules of the inner fight were simple enough: stay within the boundary of the red Photak circle, defend yourself against every trainee, ensure each one falls to the ground, and stand strong at the end.

As Yara stood in the center of the circle,

she felt herself waver. The effect of the Sleeper was growing more powerful as Pekone had warned, and with it, her strength began to wane.

"I am a Photak warrior!" she muttered harshly to herself. "A real Photak warrior!"

And it's time for them to see how I really fight, she thought smugly. She wanted them all to see what she was capable of, and her worth to the Tribe as a warrior.

Yara sunk into her own deadly stance, and a wave of reactions spread over the crowd. Yara's iridescent eyes glinted, and she felt the pulse of energy rip through her from her heartstar. She was all in now.

Out of nowhere, the first trainee swooshed in with his attack. Yara plunged straight into him without even trying to defend herself. They locked into each other with equal strength. Before he could blink, Yara spun and sank him into the ground, flittering back a little off-balance while the crowd gasped.

"ONE!" Pekone bellowed, trailing his eyes intensely on Yara.

One down and six to go, Yara thought.

Suddenly, Yara felt the burst of the Sleeper roll over her in a drowning wave.

Everything around her blurred. She stumbled and barely regained her stance. She finally understood its real power. As her heartstar pounded and pulse quickened during each fight, it would allow the poison to penetrate her system in greater sweeps. She now knew why she needed to anchor onto something that would calm her, because the faster and harder Yara went at her opponents, the more vulnerable she became for the next.

As if in response to her sobering realization, Yara felt herself slammed hard into the air and landing with a thud at the very edge of the circle. Yara felt rage fill her as the Sleeper dug into her in immediate response. Staying calm felt impossible.

No one, not even Kristos, had ever grounded Yara before.

KRISTOS, she thought.

She felt her pulse slow slightly, giving her just enough time to avoid the second trainee's brutal follow-up attack. She forced herself back on her feet and kept her thoughts on Kristos' words, repeating them like a mantra.

You are a real Photak warrior.

You are a real Photak.

I am a Photak warrior.

I am a Photak.

The anchor temporarily worked, and as the arrogant trainee attempted his third attack, Yara spun hard and fast high into the air, landing her right knee straight into his face. There would be no recovery for him.

In a rage, the third warrior-in-training roared and ran in. Yara wasn't surprised. This trainee was the rumored lover of the one before, and they were both reactive to attacks upon each other. Expecting her to do just that gave Yara an immediate advantage, and without even turning to see which direction she was coming from, Yara flipped into the air and dove back down into the lovesick trainee. Those gathered there seemed more and more anxious and upset. When the fourth and fifth trainees suffered similar fates, the inner fight status elevated.

The sixth and seventh trainees surged in from opposite sides, simultaneously. Yara felt her pulse quicken and groaned to herself as the Sleeper washed another disorienting layer of weakness over her. She could only brace herself as the double-attackers came into her, fighting even to stay upright as the world began to spin uncontrollably.

"YARA! CONCENTRATE!" she heard Kristos shout.

She could hear the panic in his voice, so she knew things were not looking good.

Pain echoed through her entire body, as blow

after blow landed on her stomach and face. She could taste her own blood now. The world around her began to shatter, and Kristos' voice began to fade.

NO, she thought desperately.

I AM A PHOTAK WARRIOR!

I AM A PHOTOK WARRIOR!

I AM A PHOTAK!

It was to no avail. The anchor was lost. Yara felt her body fracturing, along with any hope she had.

As if with a pure vengeance against Yara for her being chosen over them, the trainees did not merely throw her out the circle. Instead, they pummeled into her for what seemed like all the years she had brought chaos and discomfort to their Tribe. Yara could hardly shield herself from the battering, and she could feel the satisfaction rising from most of the onlookers. In their eyes, she was no Photak, much less a Photak warrior. She wondered why she would even think she could ever be. She could feel herself giving up and letting go.

Then at the last moment, as her eyes finally closed, as she felt them dragging her body to the circle's edge, it happened.

Chapter Four

"YaraStar... do you know who you are?"

There it was. Again. The eerie whisper of her dreams. Her body felt cold and lifeless. But the voice was alive. It called to her.

"YaraStar... do you know who you are?"

Again, and again.

"YaraStar... do you know who you are?"

It demanded her attention. With more intensity, each time.

"YaraStar... do you know who you are?"

Never louder, but with rising energy. Meaningfully. Reassuringly. Dangerously.

It was an anchor, but it was unlike anything Yara ever felt before. It was...

Power.

Pure... power.

Within that single moment, everything stopped. A single breath seemed to fill her lungs with more air than all her breathing in the sum of her life. Yara didn't stop to understand what it was or where it was coming from. All she knew was that it was making her the strongest she had ever felt.

Yara's sense of awareness kicked in. She was less than a second away from the edge, yet it was all happening in slow motion. She could see the triumphant expressions of the warriors, Kristos' crushed look of despair, the Elders' unhinged stares, and Chief Lamad's unusual disposition of shock. In all of it, she saw Pekone looking at her directly in her eyes. His eyes narrowed, and then widened, caught in an alarming moment as though he knew what was about to take place.

Yara felt the rage frenzy through her limbs and gave in to the force that overtook her body. She felt the ground become solid, and her senses heightened with indescribable clarity. She quickly pulled in her feet, crouching, her legs beneath her. Swiftly grabbing onto both trainees, she pushed and pivoted into a deadly spin. Then, in complete, flawless control, she dove herself down to the ground, slamming them both into the dirt.

Faces first.

She swung once more into the air and landed in the exact center of the red circle, crouched in her original stance, fury glinting in her eyes. She breathed heavily, and a triumphant smile edged onto her face. Whatever this energy was, it had somehow made her victorious. She had won!

Kristos cheered in jubilation, and out of the bushes somewhere, Mila squealed in delight, but as Kristos looked around him, his celebratory shouts quickly died down. Even Mila immediately stopped.

It was only then that Yara became aware of the horrified expressions of those around her. The smile left her face, and it was replaced with tortured confusion. There was silence. The kind of silence no one had ever heard before. The silence that made her realize something was very, very wrong.

The Elders turned and walked away, hissing to each other angrily as they hurried toward the main keep. Chief Lamad and the Photak warriors followed. Only the trainees remained, looking equally confused but also a bit pleased. Yara's eyes met Kristos', and he shook his head, indicating he too had no idea what had happened. He looked towards the main keep, but by now, everyone was inside. His eyes searched for any sight of his father.

No one seemed to know what to do. An inner fight usually ended with a ceremonial gifting, and the trainees were then dismissed. Everyone eventually sat on the boulders and waited patiently, knowing they could not leave before being so instructed. Within the time they waited, a couple of Photak messengers came and left but still said nothing to the trainees. Eventually, when he decided Yara probably had enough space, Kristos walked over and sat next to her in the middle of the red circle. He sighed.

"We will get answers soon, Yara," he said quietly, "but either way, everyone knows you won. You were... you were unbelievable... I don't know how... you did it..."

He paused tensely, hoping she would respond. Yara looked towards him knowing that he wanted an explanation. It was the strongest she had ever fought, the strongest she had ever felt, but she knew she had no answers to give.

"I don't really know either, Kristos..." she started slowly. "I was certain I was going to lose, but then for the first time in my life, I felt... alive... I felt... real... like I could finally feel who I am..."

Her mind flittered back to the whispering, ethereal voice that had somehow triggered the power within her. She couldn't hear it anymore, and she was a bit relieved. She felt it wiser not to mention it to Kristos as she didn't want to risk seeming crazy alongside all her other unacceptable characteristics.

"Well, whatever it was, whatever it is... you need to become it. You were powerful, Yara. You were exactly the kind of warrior this village needs."

"More powerful than you?"

A smile finally eased into her face.

"Never!" Kristos shot back, and shoved her lightly with his body.

"KRISTOS!"

Chief Lamad called out. All the trainees spun around to find the Chief walking towards them from the keep. Kristos jumped up and jogged towards him. They shared a short exchange, and Kristos turned towards Yara with a little smile. He then jogged off towards the main keep.

"Warriors-in-training," Lamad said, "you are dismissed for today. We are sorry that this day did not turn out in the way it traditionally does. The Elders and I have some deliberations to make. All will be announced and concluded at the Calling in three days."

The trainees gave each other slightly confused looks and got up to leave.

As Yara followed suit, thoughts racing, the Chief called out to her.

"Walk with me, Yara..."

***

They walked in silence through the beautiful

greenery along the village edge. Yara kept trying to brace herself for what he might have to say and wondered if she should say something first. No words came to her mind, and she felt a little intimidated.

It was the Chief who finally broke the silence.

"Yara, when your mother first brought you to us, I remember the feelings I had. You were quite a beautiful baby, with your blue hair and iridescent eyes. It was easy to see why your parents fell in love with you then. The part that I, as Chief, had to consider for the safety of my Tribe... was your unmarked skin. We had no way of knowing where you came from, or who your birth parents were. With all living things on Mira being sacredly marked, I am sure you would have understood my hesitation..."

He paused and seemed to be choosing his words with great care.

"Still, when the Elders were equally divided on keeping you, I was the one who broke the tie and said that we should. For that reason, you have always been a greater part of my responsibility…"

Lamad stopped, observing Yara to determine if she was following, and then continued.

"Today, from an objective place, you showed an incredible display of warriorship. You were triumphant in the inner fight, and under every other circumstance, it would be celebrated. The issue is…"

Lamad paused again, and Yara's heartstar pounded through her ears. The Chief was never one to have difficulty in speaking, so the fact that he was taking so much time to consider his words said enough.

"The issue is your fighting style, Yara…"

Yara felt herself breathe, almost in relief. A flurry of thoughts followed. She hadn't used the traditional Photak methods. She hadn't stuck to their traditions. She should have known this would be an issue. She secretly cursed herself for even thinking they would be impressed with her inventiveness, especially considering the nature of the Elders.

"But I still won, Chief Lamad, and I truly meant no disrespect to the Elders. I can also fight in the traditional Photak way. I just thought my own twist on it would be something you would admire."

The Chief forced a smile, but seemed sad.

"I think it was more than just a twist, Yara... Those spins were quite... non-Photak..."

"So, what does this mean then? Am I no longer automatically a warrior because of this?"

"Well..." Lamad hesitated, "the Elders have decided you will have to wait until the Calling. They will deliberate and decide by then. For now, I think you should treat this like every other trainee and continue to prepare for the next couple days."

Yara sighed and stared at the ground for a few moments, and then looked up suddenly.

"Where is Kristos? Perhaps, he and I will

train some more. It should take my mind off of all this."

The Chief's face echoed with many emotions.

"Kristos... won't be around for the next couple days. Because he is the next Warrior-in-Chief to be trained to take my place when I pass on, he is now required to undertake a much... harder... test in order to pass the Calling. The responsibilities of a Chief are very serious. You will see him at the Calling but not before then. He must take this journey alone."

"I don't understand," Yara responded with her brows furrowed. "Isn't he next in line? Is it possible for him to not be Called?"

"Yes, actually," Chief Lamad replied softly, "if he does not pass this trial and commit fully to the Call of the Chief, our birthline can be discontinued and a new line chosen from the warriors..."

Yara gasped at this realization, never knowing the pressure and responsibility that Kristos bore upon himself. Still, she had complete faith in his abilities.

"There is no way Kristos will fail," Yara confidently remarked. "There is no trial he can't endure and conquer. Don't worry, Chief, Kristos has this!"

The Chief placed a gentle hand on her shoulder and gave a small smile. He turned and walked away. Yara watched him for some time as he walked back towards the keep and then slowly started back towards her dwelling. Before she could take three steps, a shadow flew into the air from a nearby group of boulders and plunged down towards her.

Yara swung in the air and grabbed onto a laughing Mila, catching her safely as she landed back on the ground. They both laughed heartily, and Mila hugged Yara tightly. It took a few seconds before Yara realized that Mila's laughs had turned to little sobs.

"Mila! What's wrong?!"

"It's not fair, Yara! It's not fair how they cheated you! I heard what the Chief told you. The Elders are STUPID! You won FAIR AND SQUARE!"

Mila broke into sobs again.

"Aww, MilaStar..."

Yara sat on the ground and held her tightly, even more angry with herself for not sticking to the Photak fighting ways. She didn't consider how much this would also mean to Mila. She could barely stand to know she made Mila cry.

"I'm sorry, Mila. I broke the rules it seems..."

"What rules?!" Mila shot back angrily. "There are no rules about how you should fight! There are only four rules, and you kept all of them!"

Yara sighed. It was difficult to explain the concept of a generally accepted traditional rule to a child who was just as naturally defiant as Yara's blue hair. Yara had to admit, though, that deep within her she agreed with Mila. It shouldn't matter. Perhaps, her unique fighting style could even be taught to Photaks as a greater weapon against the Skotads. Traditions were a stifling thing. No one knew that better than Yara.

Yara and Mila sat in silence for a little while again, finding comfort in each other's presence. Yara had initially wanted to vent to Kristos, but these moments with Mila felt like it was what she really needed. Mila's care was pure and unadulterated. She could only hope the years ahead wouldn't change that. Mila would start her training to be a warrior as soon as she turned eight later that year.

Cognizant of the time and of Mila's mother, May, Yara gently raised Mila up and looked into her eyes.

"Okay, Mila. Today didn't go as we both hoped it would. But it's not over. The Calling is still ahead, and I've spent the past eight years training for this. I'll be a warrior a little later than we planned. Is that okay with you, young trainee?"

"I guess," Mila replied rolling her eyes but couldn't help bursting into a smile.

***

As they walked back towards the dwellings, Mila chatted excitedly about all the things Yara would be able to do when she was a warrior, especially being able to afford a piece of sensopa.

"And you must share half of it with me!" she said cheekily.

"And what about Kristos? Does he get any?"

"No!" Mila shouted as she ran down her trail to her dwelling. "Because he's a dumb boooy!"

Yara laughed as she walked on. Her belly grumbled at the thought of food. She quickened her steps. She was sure her mother would have something warmed in the heated glass, but she was also dreading having to share the details of the day. She didn't want to disappoint her parents. As she walked up to the door of her dwelling, she calmed herself knowing that her parents' love had always been unconditional.

Yara could hear her parents speaking in low voices just as she entered. She could not make out their words, but she could sense the depth of their concern.

"Yara!" Lana exclaimed and grabbed Yara into her arms for the tightest hug.

"Are you okay, YaraStar?" Sorin stood up and gently embraced her, then stood back studying her face.

"I guess I'm okay..."

"Yara... where did you learn to fight like that?" her father asked softly.

Yara glanced at both her parents, realizing only then that they already knew. Word did spread quickly in the village, and she had taken some time to come back home. She felt a bit cheated that she didn't get to share her side of it first.

"I didn't mean to disrespect the traditional style, Father," Yara complained slightly. "But, isn't it about time that the Photaks learned new ways of fighting? The methods I invented may not be how it is usually done, but if I teach the other trainees, perhaps we can defeat the Skotads once and for all! And I won, Father, did they tell you that? Mother, I won! It was an amazing fight. No one could predict my moves, and just when I thought it was the end, I felt this surge of energy and spun into the air in a flying—"

"YARA!"

Her mother stopped her with an almost panicked look on her face, and her eyes wider than Yara had ever seen before. Lana put her hands over her mouth and paced.

"Sorin, what do we do? She didn't know. It isn't her fault. Who knows what they will decide?"

"Mother," Yara said in confusion, "Chief Lamad spoke to me afterward. I will still become a warrior through the Calling. Why are you so worried about this?"

"He spoke to you?" Sorin asked. "What did he say? What did the Elders say?"

"Nothing much…" Yara said, slightly annoyed at the big deal her parents seemed to be making out of this.

It was not the reaction she expected, and it certainly lacked the comforting she needed.

"He seemed to think that I should have stuck to the traditional Photak fighting style. The Elders were disrespected by my inventiveness and—"

"Were those his exact words, Yara?"

Sorin's interruptions and Lana's pacing finally got to Yara.

"Why are you all being this way? You kept me as a baby even though I looked like a freak, but because I have a different fighting style that is way better than any Photak method, you are upset? I thought you would be proud of me! I created something that even Kristos thinks is amazing!"

Lana's expression was so horrified that Yara

stormed off into her room. Lana looked at Sorin with fear rippling on her face and tears coming to her eyes.

"They didn't tell her, Sorin… they didn't tell her she fights like a Skotad!"

Chapter Five

Yara lay in her swaddling, unable to sleep. Her parents had continued to talk in hushed, worried tones for hours after she stomped to her room. It made her feel like a complete outcast for the first time in her life. Her dwelling had always been a safe space where she felt unconditionally loved and accepted. Now, she felt like she was too much, even for her parents.

They aren't my real parents anyway, she silently

countered.

She immediately felt guilty for even thinking like that given all they had sacrificed for her. She may have felt angry with them, and everyone and everything, but most of all, she felt angry with herself. She had been so overconfident in her ability to impress the Elders and the Chief that all she had ended up doing was bringing more negative attention to how much she stuck out. She had let her ego get the best of her, and she hated herself for it. She harshly wiped the tears from her face that had managed to escape her eyes. Yara felt crying was not something becoming of a warrior.

If I ever become a warrior, she thought bitterly.

The reaction of her parents to her creativity made her feel like this was far worse in the Elders' eyes than she had initially presumed. She felt tortured by the prospect. She had never considered the possibility of life as anything other than a Photak warrior.

Her mind drifted back to the fight itself, to the voice. She didn't want to think about it, but there was something undeniably curious about its whispers. It was the way she felt when she heard it speak... Something about that intrigued her the most.

In her present, ostracized moments, its eerie call felt alluring. She wanted to beckon it somehow, and understand it more, but she felt like that was an even more dangerous indulgence. She was already facing the consequences of her unacceptable appearance and the apparent sins of her pride. She didn't need yet another incident to make her a bigger freak in everyone's eyes. She committed to herself, there and then, to never listen to the strange, ethereal voice ever again. Whatever it was, it would only make her life worse.

"Never again..." she muttered firmly, finally falling asleep.

***

"WHAT ARE YOU?!"

"WHERE DID YOU COME FROM?"

"She's such a freak."

"She's no warrior!"

"She doesn't even fight like us."

"She'll never be one of us."

"Sunstar didn't even give her markings."

"Even Sunstar knows she's a freak."

"Everyone hates you!"

"You don't belong here!"

"She should just leave."

"What is she?"

"YaraStar... do you know who you are?"

"YaraStar... do you know who you are?"

"YaraStar... do you know who you are?"

"YARA!"

Yara awoke suddenly to her father's shout

and found both of her parents standing over her swaddling, looking even more worried than the night before.

"What...?" Yara mumbled, still half asleep.

"Yara... what language were you speaking? You were moaning and crying before we woke you..."

"What..."

Yara's eyes shot open. The language! The strange one she didn't know but could somehow understand. She must have been repeating it in her sleep when she heard it in her dreams.

She became self-consciously aware of how wet her clothes were. She had been perspiring so much that her swaddling was soaked. She then remembered her parents were still waiting for a response and looked towards them. She felt ashamed when she observed them for the first time in a long time. There were signs of stress and aging that she had never noticed before. Had she been the cause of it? She couldn't help but wonder.

"I don't know, Father..." she said softly. "I think I just had a bad dream..."

Lana looked towards Sorin with a sense of grave concern.

"Yara," she said, "go on and get cleaned up. Your father and I would like to talk to you before you head out today."

Yara nodded, and as her parents left the room, she lay back and closed her eyes. She felt like she had been untethered from her usual sense of calm. Even worse, whatever this voice was, it didn't like to be ignored. She had awoken her Tribe parents because of it. She felt drained, disoriented, and tense. Yara sighed with a sense of hopelessness. There were no answers yet to explain whatever this was, and she needed to accept that for the time being.

She got up and readied herself for the day. A day in the Soar, practicing the traditional Photak fighting methods, could be the refocusing exercise she needed. She had a lot she needed to take out on the feathered trees, given that Kristos wouldn't be around to spar. Plus, now that she had her Guiding Thread, perhaps she could take a peek into the Greens. It would be her first time back there since she had been found as a baby.

Before anything, she needed to deal with her parents.

As she made her way out of her room and into the wooden, carved living space, her eyes widened in awe. There, on the table in the middle of the room, was an entire sensopa surrounded by choice picks from the beautiful flora of Mira. Her parents stood on either side of it with nothing but love in their eyes.

"Mother... Father... how did you afford..."

Her father walked over and placed his hands on her shoulders.

"Yara, there will never be a moment in your

life that we aren't proud of you. We've had this for you since yesterday, whether or not you were chosen, whether you won or lost. We were not going to wait until the Calling because we wanted you to know that we are so impressed with you, not because you may be a warrior, but because of who you are. We're sorry that yesterday did not turn out as we had planned it to... Your mother and I were very worried about you. We wish to explain why, but first, let's eat together, and you can tell us all about the inner fight... through your exquisite eyes."

Relief flooded through Yara's body as she embraced her Tribe parents and melted in the warmth of their love. They sat together and ate, each savoring every bite of the rare treat. Yara excitedly told them the details of the past day, in just the way she would have wanted. Naturally, she excluded all accounts of the troublesome voice. Despite their apparent reservations, her parents were genuinely proud, and it showed all over their faces. Only the strongest were known to win the inner fight, and considering the harder road Yara had to walk all her life, it was definitely worthy of praise.

Lana looked at Yara and smiled. She recalled their first moments together by the Sapstream in the Greens.

"You know, Yara... yesterday was sixteen years to the day since I found you as a wee one. Your father and I were already beginning to grow old, and we had given up on having a chance to fill our home with this kind of love. Still, I prayed to Sunstar for a child every single day."

Lana always retold the story on days when she felt that the family needed to be closer. She once said she believed it reminded them of how special it was that they found each other. She continued, reaching her hand towards Yara.

"It was Sunstar who showed me where you lay on the banks of that rare Sapstream. Sapstreams are unpredictable, changing their courses all the time, so to find one was a clear blessing from Sunstar. Just as a peaceful feeling of warmth overcame me, I saw a small glow of light through the Shadows and followed it to find you, my swaddled baby Yara."

Lana had never been able to conceive, and although she was worried that the baby could be a Skotad, she felt like Sunstar's signs were too great to ignore.

"I took you to the edge of the Greens. There, I slowly unwrapped your swaddling to see your reaction to Sunstar's rays. That's when I first saw your stunning blue hair—I was so shocked! I was also a little more worried then. Yet, when Sunstar's rays had touched your skin, you smiled in glee! You finally opened your eyes... They looked so strikingly beautiful, I wondered if I was dreaming!"

Yara rolled her eyes as she always did when her parents complimented her. She often joked that all parents had to say that about their children.

"When I carried you back to the village, I was

so scared that the Tribe would take this blessing, take you, away from me... but I always knew your father would support me and love you as much as I did."

Sorin reached over and held Lana's hand, his face softening in recognition of the memory.

"Those times were very difficult," Lana continued, "and if it had not been for Chief Lamad, we would have taken you and left the village... because there was no way we could imagine a life without our blue-haired belle. Thank Sunstar that the day before I found you, Kristos was born. Lamad, knowing how much it meant to him to finally have his own child, took pity on us. He placed his title, his Chiefdom, on the line for us with the promise that he would watch over you. They were all so afraid, but he wasn't. He saw that you were an innocent child blessed to walk in the light of Sunstar..."

Lana's voice broke a little. As she regained her composure, Sorin stepped in.

"We owe you an explanation for our extreme concern last night, Yara. You see... there is a lot you don't yet know about the Tribe... not because you appear to be different but because young'uns aren't allowed to be involved in the serious matters of the Tribe... and, even for us, there are still some secrets that are reserved only for the Elders and the Chief. It is Photak Law and Photak Law is the will of Sunstar."

"Is that why no one would ever talk to us about how a Skotad really looks or moves or talks or eats or anything?" Yara interrupted, bursting with curiosity.

There had been many days she and Kristos would theorize about what Skotads were like and how they fought. They had heard rumors about their pale, ghostly skins and silvery-white hair, and would often bother their trainers for answers. Their trainers would tell them to concentrate instead on mastering Photak attacks and defenses with precision first and, after the Calling, learn how to endure the Blurry in the Greens. Then and only then could they concentrate on strategically learning the Skotad methods. Those who were able to endure the Blurry the fastest and see the clearest were given the top missions for the Tribe against the Skotads. She and Kristos had dreamed about being in that leading platoon for years.

Yara noticed her parents exchanging furrowed glances. She knew there was something she was missing. Something important. Something she needed to know. She reached out and held both their hands.

"Just tell me..."

***

Deep within the main keep, Kristos lay staring at the sacred marks upon the ceilings. Yara's father had been the one to carve this particular room, as was evidenced by the mastery in the workmanship. He admired both of Yara's parents.

They were good, hardworking Photaks… and they were brave…

Kristos sighed and turned to his side, squeezing his eyes tight hoping to shut out his newfound knowledge. In fact, he didn't even consider it knowledge. It was speculation, plain and simple. Or so he desperately wanted to believe. Years of training side by side with Yara were being forcefully tainted overnight by the Elders. He had been interrogated for so many hours that he had lost track of time. Now, their training sessions at the Soar and his knowledge of her fighting style were being painted as him possibly harboring a…

No, he thought, *not Yara. They don't know her like I do… no one does…*

He swore under his breath as he felt a pang in his heartstar. He felt torn and so confused.

No Skotad had ever been able to withstand the rays of Sunstar. Even the Elders could not deny this. They had no answers as to how she could, but the fact that she fought in an advanced Skotad style meant something was wrong. It was such a superior display of strength that no Photak warrior, not even the greatest of them, had ever witnessed anything like it. Yara was seen as a serious threat. They seemed divided on the course of action to take. Some wanted to leave her and observe, turning Kristos into a spy. Others wanted to bring her in and "interrogate" her. If she did not come in willingly, they would bring her in using the ways they usually captured Skotads. Merciless ways.

Kristos shuddered at the thought. He would quicker volunteer to be a spy than let Yara ever go through that. He imagined the betrayal Yara would feel if he volunteered. She would prefer to go down fighting than understand why he needed to choose the lesser of the two evils. He shook his head as he contemplated her stubborn nature and groaned. She wasn't going to make this easy. In fact, none of this was easy.

Kristos now knew of his father's true sacrifice sixteen years ago, when he risked the Chiefdom line so that Yara's parents could keep Yara. He felt a deep sense of grief. It wasn't just the possibility of no longer becoming the next Chief that tortured Kristos. Lamad had taken on a responsibility that could cost him everything. If the Elders determined that the Chief's decisions risked the safety of the Photak Tribe, he could be excommunicated in the worst of ways. His father would be sentenced to Light Banishment. He would be sent into the Greens to succumb to the Light Blindness, never to be a part of the Photak Tribe ever again.

There was no easy solution and no foreseeable way out of this. All Kristos knew was that he wanted, and needed, to see Yara. The Elders had ordered that all communication with her should be reported directly to them in full detail. He was not even allowed to share it with his father. It was, he was told, Kristos' only way of possibly saving

Lamad from Light Banishment. Kristos decided he would find a way to fix this and prove to everyone that Yara was a Photak, not just to try to save his father, but also because…

Because I… love her…

Chapter Six

As Kristos neared the Soar, he could hear her. He winced for the poor feathered trees that were the object of her attacks. He could tell from the sounds that Yara was at the height of her anger. He realized that she must know that her fighting style was being seen as Skotad style. He hoped she knew he hadn't known. He wondered how she must have felt, especially as the Skotads were the very ones who had almost killed her Tribe mother.

He felt his heartstar pang again. It happened every time his love for Yara surfaced from the place he had shoved it down all his life.

When Kristos had stopped denying to himself that he was secretly in love with Yara, it had devastated him. He was only thirteen years old then, and he went to his father to share the sorrowful news. As the next in line to be Chief, Kristos was generally required to choose a mate from a high-born Photak line. Kristos' mother had come from such a line, but she had passed away from illness when Kristos was just a few years old. His father had been lucky as they had been very much in love. Her passing had broken Lamad for a long time.

Kristos knew what the Elders expected of his mating, but he lamented to his father that he did not want to be with a girl he did not love. Even more, he wanted to be with Yara and no one else. His father sat him down and explained the grave responsibility of a Chief and the need to bear strong children to continue the Chiefdom. His father always liked Yara's spirit, but he felt Kristos would risk a lot to take Yara as his mate. Kristos didn't know back then how much his father had already risked.

"Is there really no possible way?" Kristos asked.

His father never responded with a definite answer, but he had hinted one thing.

"If Yara becomes a Photak warrior, who knows what could be possible…" he had said.

Kristos had held on to that sliver of hope ever since.

As he quietly entered the Soar, he observed Yara's impassioned attacks with sadness. It was unusual for him, or anyone, to be able to sneak up on her. His heartstar panged again. He knew she was not okay.

"Yara…"

Yara paused upon hearing him, breathing heavily, but never turning to face him. Her arms dropped to her side. Kristos could see hints of blood on her hands. She had been at this for hours.

"What are you doing here?" she eventually asked softly.

Her voice sounded cold. Cold and hopeless.

"Oh, Yara..."

Kristos walked up to her and stood behind her. He gently rested his hand on her shoulder. Her shoulders were heaving. She was holding back tears.

"WHAT are you doing here, Kristos? Your father said you weren't to be seen until the Calling. So, why? Why are you here?"

Kristos didn't answer. He couldn't. He felt like there was nothing he could possibly say to ease her suffering. He kept his hand on her shoulder and eventually willed himself to place the other.

Yara spun in anger, swinging to attack him. As her watery eyes saw his face, she crumpled instead into his arms. A broken sob released from deep within her. Her body shook in pain.

Kristos held her tightly and felt a flood of emotion overcome him. He couldn't understand how anyone would think that Yara could ever be an evil Skotad. Skotads were senseless murderers. They attacked without provocation because of their jealousy of the Photaks' ability to dwell in Sunstar's rays. Yara was there in the rays with him, her perfect skin gleaming… a beautiful warrior, broken by the judgments of the Elders. Rage filled Kristos.

"They're wrong, Yara. They're wrong, and we'll prove it! We will show them you belong here—"

Yara shoved him back violently, her face contorted with anger.

"Prove it? Show them I belong?" she spat. "What do you think I have been trying to do my ENTIRE LIFE?!"

"Yara, I didn't mean—"

"No. NO. I have done everything, EVERYTHING, to show them that I am loyal to the

Tribe! It was not enough. It will NEVER be enough! So, don't come here now pretending like you even think I still have a chance to be a Photak warrior..."

Yara looked away in clear pain from saying aloud the words that represented the one thing she had wanted all of her life. The one thing she was certain she had now lost...

Kristos felt helpless. He already knew there was no hope for her to become a warrior at the Calling... but to give up on that possibility meant he was giving up on so much more. He sighed in exasperation. The only way to save his father was to prove that Lamad had not made a mistake with Yara. It was also the only way he could...

"We can't give up, Yara. You can't give up. Not now. Not when we're this close."

"Why do you even care, Kristos?" Yara shot back bitterly. "You are going to have everything you ever wanted. Becoming a Photak warrior. Becoming the Chief!"

"Not everything…" Kristos replied softly.

Yara laughed sarcastically.

"Oh, there is more? That's not enough for you? What more could you possibly want in this world?!"

Kristos brows furrowed. He turned to face Yara. His jaw was rigid and his face taut with determination. He stared deeply into her eyes.

"You, Yara… I want… you…"

***

Yara felt the world begin to spin around her. She was sure she couldn't have possibly heard those words come from Kristos' lips. Her mind was already unhinged with all that her parents had told her. Could Kristos have just declared that he wanted her as his mate? Still? Despite everything? It was impossible. Yet, he stood in front of her, searching her eyes and face for some kind of response.

Yara stared down at the ground. Her body trembled slightly. Kristos gently extended his arm, putting his finger beneath her chin and raising her face.

She locked eyes with him, and for the first time, she saw how much he cared. His walls were down, and from behind them came a tidal wave of love. She immediately felt even angrier with herself for the way she had fought the inner fight. She knew there was no way he could take her as a mate after what had happened. Not if he wanted to be the Chief. There was no way she would let him give that up for her. Bitterness overwhelmed her.

"Well… it doesn't matter now, does it?"

Her response seemed to anger Kristos.

"Yara, did you even hear what I said? I said I want you. I want you, Yara. I love…"

Yara's look of horror seemed to stop Kristos short, but he shook his head and looked her dead in her eyes.

"I love you, YaraStar. I have for a very long time. So, don't tell me it doesn't matter now…

because now, it's all that matters."

"Yeah, okay, you love me, I love you, and suddenly all is well with the world?! Sure, you love me… but do you love me enough to defy the Elders? Love me enough to give up the Chiefdom?! You don't, so this doesn't change anything. It just makes it worse!"

Kristos' eyes blazed with fiery care at Yara's declaration of returned love. He didn't seem to hear anything else she had to say. He stepped toward her and grabbed her with passionate strength. He cupped her face in his hand, breathing heavily as emotions stormed over his face. Then, he sunk his lips deeply into hers.

Yara's heartstar pounded in her chest. She felt all her pores rise and her resolve immediately weaken. For a moment, she let herself feel it… feel all that she had ever wanted. For an indescribable moment, Kristos was finally hers. It felt like she had been thrown high into the air…

But then came the fall.

"YaraStar... do you know who you are?"

Yara's eyes flew open, and she stumbled back. It was here again, audibly speaking to her.

"YaraStar... do you know who you are?"

Yara squeezed her eyes shut, overwhelmed with frustration. She slammed her hands over her ears trying to block out the voice, but it didn't stop. Then, she realized. The voice wasn't speaking to her, it was speaking from her. It was on the inside of her mind. It was all so much, it was all too much.

"LEAVE ME ALONE!" she shouted desperately at it. Yara left, running out of the Soar.

In that moment, she didn't even remember that she was leaving behind a bewildered and pained Kristos.

***

Yara ran faster and harder than she ever had before. Tears streamed down her face and flew off into the wind. Her body moved with heated strides, and her feet barely touched the ground before lifting off again. She could no longer hear the voice, but she still kept running. She ran without stopping, without thinking… at least until she reached the edge of the Greens. It was there she slammed to a stop, panting as she hunched over with her hands on her knees. As her breathing evened, she stood up straight and looked around her.

With a rush, the memory of what had just happened overwhelmed her. Her hand flew over her mouth as a little cry escaped. She had left Kristos there, just as he had declared his love for her. What else could she have done, she wondered… and what was she to do? She couldn't tell him about the voice. She couldn't let him give up the Chiefdom. She wanted this so badly. It was an impossible situation.

Suddenly, Yara felt her senses heighten.

There was always a prickly sense of danger closer to the Greens' edges. She squinted and stared into the Shadows. Subconsciously, she reached toward her pocket. She could feel the Guiding Thread there, and she felt her heartstar skip a beat.

This is stupid, Yara, she thought to herself, *you're already in enough trouble as is.*

Yet somewhere within her, she wondered. What if she could still become a warrior... what if she could still have... him?

It was a bad idea and she knew it. Capturing a Skotad to prove her loyalty would be no easy feat. She had very little time before the day of the Calling and no experience in the Greens. She had never even seen a Skotad before. Still, she somehow figured, today she could practice with the Blurry, tomorrow she could capture a Skotad, and the next day she could finally prove herself to the Tribe. It may have been unrealistic, but it was all that she had.

With brazen determination, Yara tied one

end of her Guiding Thread to a tree at the edge of the Greens. She tugged at it to make sure it was secure. Then, with a deep breath, she turned and took her first step into the Greens. The air immediately felt thicker and a little sticky. Yara squeezed her hand around the Thread and took a few more steps. She loved the soft glow it gave off and felt admiration for Pekone's skills in making it. As she ventured further away from the edge, Yara gasped.

All she felt was awe. The Greens were alive with flora that she had never seen before. Their colors were bright and rich, and everything seemed to thrive in joy. In the distance ahead, she saw a tree that looked old and magical. She recognized it from her training to be one of the many Saptrees of the Greens. Its branches called to her, dancing in waves, almost as though they were happy for the company in the lonely woods.

She exclaimed in glee and ran swiftly to it. Upon reaching it, she embraced its soft, marked trunk with pleasure. She could see the paths of sapjuice through its semi-transparent upper layer. She peeled back a bit of its skin and put her lips over the tear. She drank the sapjuice from it gratefully as all her running had brought on great thirst. After she had her fill, she sat upon its soft roots and sighed. She felt a little guilty about her tinges of happiness from being able to see the beauty of the Greens. It was something she and Kristos had often talked about doing together.

After a little while, Yara felt refreshed and rested. She surveyed the surroundings. Her eyes landed on a mushroom patch a bit further in. She grinned. Those particular mushrooms were very valuable in her village. Her parents would be thankful, and she could now pay them back for the costly sensopa they had gotten for her celebration.

She got up, subconsciously tugging her Guiding Thread, ensuring it was still firmly connected. Taking one last gulp of sapjuice from the Saptree's trunk, Yara turned to make her way towards the patch. After three steps, she froze. Her eyes were fixed. She felt her body begin to quiver. Every pore on her skin rose, and horror crept up her spine. So… much… horror. Her eyes widened as panic gripped her body.

No…

"NO!"

Chapter Seven

Yara ran as fast as her strong legs could take her, even quicker than she had before. Her arms flashed quickly in front of her as she sped along the path of the Guiding Thread. She flew past the edge of the Greens into the clearing, stopping for a moment and looking wildly around her. Then, she didn't stop running... not until she reached the Soar. She needed privacy from the village, from everyone. She needed to process what had just happened. As she entered, she fell on her hands and knees, breathing heavily.

Everything blurred around her, but it was the kind of blur that she hated. She raised her head, causing the welled-up tears that clouded her vision to drop from her eyes. It brought much needed clarity. There, still there, was Kristos. He paused, seeming shocked and concerned, then shot up. He began to make his way towards her from the boulder upon which he had been sitting.

Her thoughts raced. She knew she probably needed to talk to him, but she didn't yet have the words to explain it. Unable to face him, she pushed herself up, stumbling away from him as he drew near.

"I'm sorry," she said, tears welling up in her eyes again. "I can't..."

This time, she went all the way to her dwelling. She flew into her room and flung herself into her swaddling. She was grateful that no one was there as she could no longer hold back her weeping. Her swaddling barely muffled the sounds of her sobs. They ripped through her as the terror continued to torture her mind.

She heard a husky voice call out softly from the outside of her dwelling. Kristos had followed her. She could not see the way his fists clenched or his legs paced, but she could hear the pained care in his words.

"What's wrong, Yara? What happened?!"

He begged her to talk to him, but all she could do was cry. Eventually, she got herself to form a few coherent words.

"Leave me be, Kristos. I can't. I just can't right now. Please... just leave me be..."

She heard the rustling of the grass as he slowly walked away, kicking his feet in defiant disagreement with every step.

***

By the time Yara's Tribe parents came back

to the dwelling, she was numb to it all. She lay on the swaddling staring at the sacred markings above her. They were the same markings in every dwelling, from every Saptree, in symbols no one ever seemed to fully understand. Some said they told of the time before the Great War, when there was day and night, light and darkness. Some said they showed that both the Photaks and the Skotads came from the same ancestors. Others said it proved Sunstar's blessings upon the Photaks.

Lana was the first to realize Yara was in the dwelling. She was bringing fresh swaddling to Yara's room and was startled by her presence.

"Well, in all my years I am certain that this is the first time I've seen you here at this time, YaraStar," she teased as she walked in.

"I decided to make it an early day..."

On seeing Yara's forced smile, Lana put down the swaddling quietly. Then, she lay down next to her. They were quiet for a little while, and then Yara turned to her.

"Mother... do you think I'm really a Photak?"

Lana seemed taken aback by the question but seemed to assume that the inner fight was on Yara's mind. She turned to face Yara, gently stroking a few blue strands that had slid across Yara's brilliant eyes. She sighed sadly.

"The truth is... I don't know, my sweet girl... but here is what I do know: you... are NOT a Skotad..."

Lana looked steadily into her eyes with loving reassurance, but the flash of doubt that crossed Lana's face for a fleeting moment did not escape Yara's probing.

"How do you KNOW that, Mother...? How can anyone know...?"

Lana looked away slightly as the distressing memory of her Skotad encounter entered her mind.

"When I was attacked, you were only six years old. I was out gathering mushrooms in the

Greens from a beautiful patch I had found the day before. Our warriors were nearby, as they always were, watching over the perimeter in which we were gathering."

Lana paused and frowned slightly.

"I never saw him. I was bent over picking from one of the patches when something hit me extremely hard on my head. I don't know how long I was unconscious, but when I awoke, I could barely move. One of our warriors lay nearby. He had a Skotad arrow in his chest. He was probably killed trying to save me. I had been left for dead."

Yara could barely breathe as her Tribe mother spoke. She had never told her the real story of what had happened. Yara reached her arm over Lana as she continued.

"I kept going in and out of consciousness, too weak to move. I tried crawling so many times, but the pain would knock me right out again. The hours turned to days. Soon, I was certain that it had been almost three days as my eyes were starting to clear from the Blurry. The Light Blindness was beginning. I was terrified... terrified to never dwell in Sunstar's light, to never see you and Sorin again..."

Lana's voice broke a little as she considered how close she had come to losing everything she had ever loved.

"Then I heard them in the distance... our warriors. They were calling out my name, but they were so very far. I tried to respond, but my throat was dry, and I couldn't speak. Suddenly, for the second time in my life... a Sapstream appeared... just like the one by which I had found you. It came flowing by, and as it passed me, it branched out... It brought its waters right to my lips, and I drank until I could finally speak. Then, it went in the direction of the warriors, carrying along my blue scarf on its currents. It found them. They followed the Sapstream back... back to find me."

Yara's eyes were wide with wonder. The

sacred Sapstreams had helped the warriors find her mother… just like they had helped Lana find her.

"You see, Yara, I KNOW you are Sunstar's gift to me… and I KNOW you are not a Skotad. You could NEVER be so senselessly evil and attack someone who is defenseless. You are not a Skotad, not only because you can walk in Sunstar's light… but also because you have such a good heart, my YaraStar."

Lana wrapped her arms around Yara, hugging her tightly, and for the first time in the past day, Yara felt calmer. She did not want to tell her mother what had happened. She felt like her parents had enough to worry about from her inner fight. Still, she knew there was one person to whom she owed an explanation. Right now, though, all that mattered was being with her Tribe mother.

She pulled away from Lana and touched her face, eyes filled with love.

"Thank you for telling me all of this. I love

you, Mother… you, and Father."

***

The next day, Yara left the dwelling and made her way back to the Soar. She hoped Kristos would be there. She felt calmer after her mother's reassuring words the day before. Perhaps, what she had discovered in the Greens had another explanation. She desperately needed someone to talk to… someone she could completely trust.

She could see Kristos sitting right on the same boulder from where he had witnessed her shameful display of tears. He seemed to be deep in thought, and very troubled, but as he noticed her approaching, relief flooded over his face.

Yara walked up to him and then perched on a tuft of grass facing him. She stared at him, unsure of how to begin speaking. So instead, she let her eyes drift along his face and body, absorbing details that were both familiar, yet so different. She had never really noticed that he looked so much more mature now than when they were kids. He was becoming a man. His skin and markings seemed to glow with Sunstar's light, revealing waves of muscles that twitched with strength. His brown eyes peered deeply when she finally allowed hers to meet his again.

"Talk to me..." he whispered.

She took a deep breath. Then, it all came rushing out like a flood. She told him about her decision to go into the Greens, about how amazing the glow of the Guiding Thread was, about seeing the Saptree and the refreshing moment she had, and about her spotting the exquisite mushroom patch. His eyes lit up with many emotions... fear that she went in alone, excitement for what she had seen, pride at her bravery, and then confusion.

"These all seem to be amazing experiences, Yara..."

"I know... but it's what happened next..."

She gazed down at the pocket that held her

Guiding Thread.

“One mile… Our first issue Threads are always one mile long… right?”

“Yes…?”

“Kristos… the Saptree was one mile in… my Thread… it was finished. I didn’t even notice… I was so caught up in the moment…”

She paused at Kristos’ perturbed then angry expression.

“You went in the entire mile?! On your first time?! How could you even see? Yara, that’s so dangerous! Not even Pekone could handle the blurring for an entire mile in on his first time! WHAT were you thinking?!”

Kristos was no longer holding back the extent of his care for Yara. She could feel the layered concern in his words. It warmed her strangely… but it made her hesitant to continue.

Be brave, Yara, she told herself.

“Well… that’s just it. I didn’t feel a thing…

as in, I never… I never had any blurring…"

"What…?"

"I don't know how to explain it… I think I could have gone further… but then I realized I had no more Thread left…"

Her eyes brimmed with tears.

"I thought I had experienced Light Blindness, Kristos! I thought if I could see so clearly in the Greens, it meant I couldn't be in Sunstar anymore. But I ran back out, and I was fine… I was fine… I don't know what it means, but…"

With the rest of her resistance giving way to her outpouring, she willed herself to say the words that scared her the most.

"I can see… I can see clearly in the Shadows…"

Chapter Eight

Kristos stared at Yara in complete confusion and, with it, hints of fear. What she was saying was not rational... It was not possible. He gazed at her, uncertain how to respond to what she had said. Only Skotads, and Light Blinded Photaks, could see clearly in darkness... but they definitely could not also dwell in Sunstar's light. Yet, somehow, Yara could do both.

The rays of Sunstar caused Yara's iridescent

eyes to gleam as she earnestly waited on his response. Kristos could see their sparkling colors... yellows, reds, and golds with specks of blues and greens. For the first time, Yara's eyes didn't seem quite as mesmerizing. They now felt... strange... to him. They felt slightly suspicious. Guilty pangs shot through him. This was Yara. Yara, the girl that he had known his entire life, the girl he loved. Still, as he looked over her unmarked skin, he wondered...

What... is she...

His thoughts ran to his father. Chief Lamad had risked everything to let Lana and Sorin keep Yara. Now, Kristos was the only chance his father had at being saved. How could he save him if he couldn't prove that Yara was a Photak?

"Kristos... say something..."

Yara's expression began to turn to one of regret. Kristos didn't want her to feel she shouldn't have told him, but he also still didn't know how to respond.

"I'm sorry, Yara… I am still trying to process everything you're saying…"

"And I am trying to process everything that's happening to me, Kristos! You think I asked for any of this?! I'm telling you because you're the only person in this world who I can trust… because I know you will keep my secret and help me figure this out. You will, won't you? Or are you too caught up in your own shock to even care?!"

Kristos winced at her harsh words but mentally shook himself. He hadn't stopped to think about how scared Yara must be feeling. She hadn't known that any of this would even happen. Compassion filled his heartstar. For a moment, he put aside his fears for his father's life. He put himself into her shoes and understood how much her world must be falling apart.

"You're right. I really am sorry. I let the shock of what you said eclipse my commitment to you as a friend."

“A friend? So… I am no longer good enough for your love then… no longer worthy of being your mate because I can see in the Shadows…?”

“Yara, I didn’t mean—”

“Save it.”

With her curt reply, Yara got up and angrily walked away.

Kristos sighed gruffly and dropped his head into his hands. He wanted to call after her and ease her mind. He also knew he couldn’t do that without having to explain everything. How was he to tell her that if he didn’t commit to spying on her and reporting back to the Elders, he could lose his father to the darkness forever… the very darkness in which Yara could apparently see. He didn’t know how she would react, but he knew nothing good could result from it.

Added to that, Kristos was now confounded by Yara’s revelations about the Shadows. Within himself, he had never seen Yara as anything other than a differently beautiful Photak. He felt himself beginning to doubt that for the very first time. His mind ran across what one of the Elders had told him the day before.

"Yara is a Skotad weapon!" Elder Malek had said. "They found a way to help her withstand Sunstar's rays! They planted her here among us until the time was right... and that time is now! Did you see how she fought? She was the most advanced Skotad we have ever seen. They must have been training her all along! Plus, no one gets over the Sleeper like that!"

Kristos had grunted defiantly at the Elder's accusations, but now he wasn't so sure anymore. He certainly didn't think that Yara had been training with the Skotads, especially since they had spent almost every day together for the past eight years.

But what if she is a weapon, or a Skotad of some kind, and she doesn't even know it...

Kristos jumped up, suddenly aware of what

he needed to do. If he could get Pekone to decide that Yara was not a weapon, or at least not one by choice, the Elders would listen to him... because no one knew more about Skotads and their weapons than Pekone. That could be the only way to fix this, for his father and for Yara. He needed to talk to Pekone, and he needed to do it right away.

As Kristos made his way to Pekone's dwelling, he went over what he would say, again and again. Pekone lived on the far outskirts of the village, close to the most dangerous edge of the Greens. He had his dwelling built there on purpose, so he could personally ensure he was always on the frontlines for possible Skotad attacks. As Kristos walked up to the dwelling, he could see Pekone sitting on his large chair just outside, smoking his pipe. He didn't seem surprised to see Kristos.

"Young Chief, what brings you this far out of the village?"

Kristos grabbed a Saptree log that lay nearby,

turning it into a seat, and studied Pekone. He could never tell what mood Pekone was in.

"I am sure by now you know about what the Elders have asked me to do..."

"Spy on your blue-haired love in exchange for saving your father? Why yes, I'm aware..."

Kristos balked a little at Pekone's directness but willed himself to concentrate on his purpose for coming.

"Yes, they want me to report to them about Yara so that I can prove my loyalty to the Tribe... in exchange for mercy granted to my father and his vote so many years ago."

Pekone looked at Kristos with a continued blank expression, and it unnerved him a bit more.

"Why do you think the Elders see Yara as a Skotad weapon? I mean, you're the expert at weapons... so do you agree with them?"

Pekone's eyes narrowed slightly. He took a long pull through his pipe and breathed the smoke out slowly.

"A Skotad weapon...?" he drawled.

Kristos felt a small surge of annoyance, but he knew he couldn't afford to reveal his desperation.

"Yes. That's what Elder Malek said."

"Hmmm..."

He took another long pull, and Kristos felt himself getting angry.

"Unless, of course, you aren't that knowledgeable about Skotad weapons."

Pekone immediately glared at Kristos but finally gave him the answer he sought.

"I know everything there is to know about Skotad weapons. Skotads are a ruthless people, a violent people... but they aren't proficient at weaponry design... certainly not anything close to producing a weaponized baby."

Kristos grinned slightly. He saw the look of annoyance spread over Pekone's face as he realized he had been baited. Pekone continued, still glaring.

"Perhaps, the Elder found some answers in the ancient texts of Truth that substantiate his claims..."

Kristos' smile was immediately erased. If that were even remotely true, there would be nothing he could do to fix this. The ancient texts of Truth were above all other knowledge, and judgment. He knew about them only because he was the son of the Chief. The Elders and the Chief used them for reference on all things that concerned Photak Law.

"Did they? Did they find anything in them?!"

Pekone's eyes glinted with satisfaction at his reaction, but Kristos didn't care. Pekone grunted and then looked at him with unusual seriousness.

"Look... I know you wouldn't be here if you didn't need me, Young Chief. You've clearly been with Yara today, and there must be things you know. So... I'll tell you what... if you share your secrets with me, I'll share mine with you... and together we can figure all of this out."

Kristos couldn't help but feel a sense of relief at Pekone's offer. The burden of all of this was something he usually shared with his father. He felt a stab of shame knowing he was going to share Yara's secret, but he mostly felt a renewed sense of hope. Whether or not Yara would admit it, she too would know that Pekone was a powerful ally.

He told Pekone everything. He told him about their training sessions, Yara's innocence in the inner fight, her fears that anyone could ever think she was a Skotad, and even his professed love for her. Then, he told him about Yara's trip into the Greens.

Pekone's body straightened the more that Kristos shared. He leaned forward as Kristos told him Yara had used the full length of her Guiding Thread.

"The full length... the entire mile... on her very first time? Kristos, are you sure Yara hadn't already been journeying into the Greens on her own?"

"I'm certain of it," Kristos responded.

"She must have barely been able to see. I know she is a brave one, and she probably feels like she has something to prove, but that sounds like pure stupidity!" Pekone said indignantly.

"Well... that's just it... she... she never experienced the Blurry..."

Pekone's eyes narrowed.

"What did you say?"

"Yara..." Kristos stammered a little, "she... she can see in the Shadows..."

Pekone rose from his chair, gawking at Kristos. Then, he began to pace with a deadly serious look on his face. After a couple of minutes, he turned and faced Kristos.

"Where is Yara now?"

"I... I don't know... I might have angered her, and she walked off so—"

"Where do you think she would have gone?!"

“Pekone, I said… I don’t know. She roams a lot when she is upset. But why? Why do you need to know where she is? And what are your secrets? What does all of this mean?”

Pekone looked at Kristos dead in his eyes.

“It means if we don’t find Yara and get to the bottom of this before the Elders find out, your father will definitely be sent to Light Banishment. They plan to secretly judge him today, Kristos! In the next few hours! Find her. Find her and bring her to me. Find her before you lose your father forever!”

***

Yara gasped softly. Quickly, her hands shot up to cover her mouth. She couldn’t believe what Pekone had just said. As she lay hidden in the bushes, she finally understood why Kristos seemed so torn and grieved by her revelation. She had angrily returned to the Soar to tell him a bit more of her mind when she saw him walking in the distance. She realized that his direction meant there was only one place he could be going, and she fumed with even more anger. He seemed to be ready to betray her trust right away. To be certain, she had snuck up the other side of Pekone's dwelling and listened to all that was being said. She never expected what she heard.

Poor Kristos...

Her heartstar broke at the thought of the torture he must be going through. To know that in all of this he was still trying to save her along with his father, that meant the world to her. Still, she wasn't quite sure she was ready to face Pekone. Yara had found it difficult to ever trust anyone the way she trusted Kristos. She knew Kristos had left Pekone's dwelling to go search for her, but she wasn't ready to be found.

Then, as she was about to sneak away, she heard Pekone call out.

"You can come out now, you know... He's gone."

Yara felt her stomach pang, and she lowered her head. She had been so careful. No one had ever discovered her when she was in stealth mode before.

As she got up to come out, she heard another voice respond.

"Well... that was interesting..."

Then, out of the shadows of Pekone's dwelling came Elder Malek.

Chapter Nine

Tears of terror flooded Yara's eyes. Her heartstar pounded so hard that she could barely hear anything else. Her thoughts went wild with panic. Elder Malek was known to have been the strongest opposition to her Tribe parents even keeping her as a baby. He had openly accused Lana and Sorin of purposely putting the Tribe at risk. He saw her parents' defiance as a form of rebellion against the will of Sunstar. He believed that if Lana were meant to have a child, then she would have had one with Sorin. To him, Yara was a curse.

"We always knew the blue-haired abomination was a Skotad weapon. Even you can't deny it now, Pekone."

"A weapon... maybe. But a threat... definitely. I will say it is curious that she can still also survive in Sunstar's rays..."

Malek spat indignantly.

"That child's very existence defies the will of Sunstar. We have found nothing in our extensive search of the ancient texts that corroborates Lana's naive claims of signs from Sunstar."

"Well... you did find one thing..."

"Unsubstantial!" Malek sneered. "Plus, she has no markings, so it's impossible! All living things, ALL creations of Sunstar, have sacred birthlines. She must have been made by the Skotads!"

Pekone seemed to consider the possibility for the first time. He turned to the Elder as a flash of alarm crossed his face… one that Yara had never seen before.

"If that be the case, then the Tribe is in far more danger than we have estimated."

"So, find the abomination, Pekone! And find a way to ensure she speaks. Your light torches won't work on her. She must be interrogated like the Skotad she is. I am holding you personally responsible for the safety of this Tribe!"

Pekone's eyes narrowed. He didn't like to take orders. As Malek walked off, Pekone called after him in a cold, deadly tone.

"Perhaps, if you had finished the job, Elder Malek, we wouldn't be in this position. Your cowardice when the Skotad saved Lana is the reason why Sorin and Yara stayed. If you had killed her like you planned, the three days would have passed, and Sorin would have assumed that Lana had succumbed to Light Blindness. Sorin would have left with Yara in search of Lana… He would have given up Sunstar's rays for her! And if he had done that, we wouldn't be in this mess today. But don't worry... I won't be as careless as you were... No Skotad could ever get in my way."

Malek had paused while Pekone spoke, but then he continued walking, clearly deciding it wasn't worth it. Pekone went into his dwelling with an insidious laugh.

Yara covered her mouth and held back a horrified cry. She didn't believe... she couldn't believe... Elder Malek had been responsible for the attack on her mother. He was the one who had wanted her dead.

And a Skotad... saved my mother?

She felt nauseated but forced herself to check her surroundings. Even if she had the capacity to, she couldn't afford to think about this at this moment. Not when the present threat was so great. When she felt it was safe, she pushed herself up. They would be sending a search party for her soon.

She needed to go. She needed to go now.

***

Yara stole back to her dwelling, avoiding all the usual paths. She knew it was a risk even to go back there, but she couldn't just leave her Tribe parents. They needed to know she had gone, and they needed to know why.

She entered quietly even though she knew they wouldn't be there. Her mother would be out selling the mushrooms she had gathered. Her father would be in the middle of his day's work, building and carving.

She searched the dwelling and soon found a blank scroll and a feathered quill. Her hands shook as she began to write.

> Mother, Father,
> I am so sorry that I have to leave, but Malek and Pekone are after me. They are convinced I am of the Skotads and a danger to our Tribe. But they aren't what they seem, Father. Mother, Malek

planned the attack on you, in the Greens. Pekone knows. I heard Pekone say that it was a Skotad who saved you. I don't know what it all means but please don't trust them. I love you... and my thoughts will be with you, always,

YaraStar.

Yara paused, and then wrote one more line.

Also, please tell Kristos I'm sorry for everything... and I love him.

She placed the letter beside the glass wares that her mother would go to when she came back to prepare the meal. Then, she looked around for any food she could take. She opened the doors to the little storage her parents kept. In it were just a few items. It had been a hard few months.

Yara sighed and closed back the doors. She couldn't take the little food her parents had even though she knew they would want her to have all of it. She would find more than enough food in the Greens. She felt a hint of dread as she considered the perilous stories of the Greens told by the warriors. She shook it off. There was no time for second thoughts now… not with Pekone after her.

After she gathered her dagger, bow, and arrows, alongside a few other things, Yara walked toward the door. She paused, surveying her father's beautiful dwelling creation one last time. She looked towards her room and the fresh swaddling her mother had placed. This place had been her solace for all of her life. As Yara reached for the door's handle, she stared for a moment at its sacred markings. She wished she could understand what they meant.

"What am I…?" she whispered to herself.

She opened the door and stole quietly out to the shrubbery nearby. As she turned to make her way through them to the old paths, a shadow flashed before her. A cry of capture sounded in the air.

"IIIIII GOOTTTT YOUUUUUUUUUUU!"

shouted a triumphant Mila, clearly thrilled by the look of fear on Yara's face.

Yara swiftly grabbed her and pulled her into the shrubs, covering her mouth and looking around desperately.

"Shhhhhhh, Mila… stop shouting, please!" she hissed.

Mila nodded with wild eyes. Yara gently removed her hand from Mila's face.

"What's wrong, YaraStar?"

Mila's exaggerated whispering made Yara wince.

"Okay… I need you to listen, okay? Listen and don't say a word. Can you do that, Mila?"

Mila nodded silently to show she could.

Yara sighed and sat back a little. She had no idea how to explain it all to Mila, or how much she should even explain. She didn't want Mila to get in trouble. She also didn't want to break Mila's heartstar by leaving without an explanation. She had forgotten how much the little one looked up to her with all that had been happening.

"I have to go, Mila... I have to leave the village..."

Mila's face echoed with confusion. She pointed at her head to emphasize it even more.

"I know... it is a confusing time for me too. The Elders... they think my fighting style is similar to the Skotads... and they think I'm a danger to the Tribe..."

Mila savagely shook her head in disagreement. She had been spying on Yara's training for so long that she knew it just wasn't true.

"I know... but the Elders won't believe me. They are trying to capture me now, so I have to leave... I'm so sorry to leave you, Mila..."

Mila's eyes filled with tears, and she grabbed Yara, squeezing her tightly while forcefully shaking her head.

Yara felt her heartstar pang and her eyes

water.

"I'm so sorry, Mila..."

Soon, Mila looked up and pointed at her mouth, asking if she could speak. Yara nodded, reminding her she needed to be quiet.

"I don't want them to capture you, Yara. So, I know you have to go. And I know you're not a Skotad... but... even if you were a Skotad... I'd still think you're the best. You're the best, Yara. No matter what."

Yara felt passionately moved by Mila's innocence and loyalty.

"I hope I get to see you again one day, little one..." she replied, kissing Mila lightly on her forehead.

As Yara snuck away, Mila looked out to make sure no one had seen her. Their eyes made contact one last time. Yara proudly nodded before disappearing into the bushes.

***

Yara walked north towards the Greens from a different path. She concentrated solely on her mission. She needed to leave the village undetected, and she needed to put as much distance between it and her as she could before the day ended. As she neared the edge from the side the Photaks never used, she looked back in the direction of the village. A forlorn look crept over her face.

She knew that the moment she stepped into the Greens would be the moment her Photak life would be over. It was the price of her freedom, but it was at the heaviest cost imaginable. She allowed herself to think once more about her Tribe parents and their undying love. She thought about Kristos and the pain he must be feeling trying to save his father. She wished she had the time to tell him the details of Pekone's betrayal, but she was afraid to risk making things worse for him.

Yara took a huge breath and looked ahead into the Greens. She looked down, touching the

Guiding Thread in her pocket. She took it out, gazing upon it nostalgically. For years, she had been excited for the day she would finally have one. She reached out her arm and dropped it into the bushes.

"I won't be needing you anymore…" she muttered as she walked into the Greens.

***

For the next few hours, Yara headed further and further away from the village. She deliberately chose directions that she heard had sparse sustenance. While she knew food would be harder to find, she also knew there would be a smaller chance of stumbling into anyone. With the gravity of her circumstances weighing down, Yara knew it was worth the risk.

The further away she got, the more she looked ahead, instead of behind. Soon, she felt confident that she had not been followed. Only then did she allow herself to acknowledge her awe at the beauty that surrounded her. Despite the shadowy darkness, there was something about all the new sights, sounds, and smells that made her feel alive.

She felt a surreal sense of gratitude that her eyesight availed her to see in the Shadows. She could not imagine doing any of this while disabled by the Blurry. Still, it wasn't quite how she had imagined she would have experienced the Greens. She allowed her thoughts to run over the events of the past couple of days and shook her head in disbelief. A couple of days ago, her biggest problem had been the new voice that tortured her dreams.

The voice!

Yara felt an immediate surge of rage. All of this, everything bad that had happened, started because of the eerie voice. It had left her dreams to torture her in real life. While she knew that she would have lost if it hadn't helped her in the inner fight, she also knew that she would at least still have had her old life. Yara's jaw clenched the more she thought about it.

"So, where are you now, you eerie nuisance!" she said out loud. "Come on! Speak up! You sure know how to make an entrance. In the inner fight, in the middle of my first kiss!! So, make your entrance now, seeing that you've ruined my ENTIRE LIFE!"

She paused and listened for a moment. She almost expected it to respond. There was silence.

"ARGHHHH!!"

Yara kicked at a red glass-sharded stone and dropped down next to a feathered tree. She sighed and held her head. She felt like she was going quite mad. The voice probably wasn't even real, and either way, there was nothing she could do about it now.

Focus, Yara, she thought to herself, *you need to focus on surviving. So... what do you need to survive?*

She looked up at the furs of the feathered tree. She could make a mini swaddling with them. She just needed to find food and a safe place to rest. The very thought of sleep made her body ache. It had been a long day.

She pushed herself up and went searching the area. She found a low-lying canopy of branches a little way off. After a quick perimeter sweep, she felt confident that it was adequately safe. She built the makeshift swaddling. Then, she hydrated herself by a nearby Saptree and found a tiny mushroom patch for sustenance.

She returned to the swaddling and lay down for the day. She would have never known that the last time she had slept in her own swaddling would have been her very last. Yara's life had changed, drastically and mercilessly. She was drained beyond words.

Yara closed her eyes. Within minutes, the exhaustion took its hold, and she drifted off to sleep.

***

"WHAT ARE YOU?!"

"SHE'S A SKOTAD!"

"We always knew it!"

"She's such a freak!"

"Cursed abomination!"

"She's a weapon!"

"She isn't even a real person."

"She has no markings!"

"She was MADE by Skotads!"

"She doesn't belong here!"

"She doesn't belong anywhere."

"YaraStar..."

"YaraStar..."

"YaraStar... ARISE!"

Yara shot up from her swaddling, the furs falling from her as she hit her head into the canopy. She held her forehead and groaned, feeling disoriented.

What did I even hit...? she thought, trying to figure out what it was in her room back at her dwelling.

Then, it all came back in a rush. She remembered where she was and felt a shot of panic. Instinctively, she peered out from her hiding place and surveyed the surroundings. Everything looked the same, peaceful and beautiful. She calmed herself. She had taken a lot of care in choosing this place of rest. She lay back down, sighing with her hand still on her forehead, damning the voice for its continued torment.

In the distance, a steady hand that pulled back a taut bowstring with an arrow paused its release...

Chapter Ten

Toler stared in shock as he lowered his bow. His brows furrowed in confusion. Perhaps, his expertly skilled eyes had somehow deceived him, but he could have sworn the Photak had…

Blue hair…

He rubbed his eyes and stared at the place where she hid. She had lain back down now, and he couldn't see her head anymore. The low canopy kept her well concealed.

It's a brilliant hiding spot, Toler thought smugly.

He knew because he had fashioned the canopy himself. He had been returning when he saw a person wearing Photak garb had inhabited it. It seemed similar to those of the warriors. He thought, perhaps, the Photak was some kind of spy.

Regardless, a Photak of any kind was a threat. Photaks had been brutal to his people. His Tribe had lost many innocent people as a result of their hate. Photaks hunted them like animals and committed gruesome acts of torture upon their skin with weapons of light. While he never attacked or initiated fights with them, he couldn't just leave the Photak there to harm his people.

He decided to poison the tip of his arrow and graze the sleeping Photak. It would release a dosage that would be enough to disable but not to kill. He had been about to fire off the arrow when she had jumped up. She had hit her head so hard that the thud could be heard a far way off.

Nope, not a warrior, he had thought, slightly amused at her self-deprecating mutterings that followed.

As he observed her now, he wondered where she had come from and why she was so far away from her village. This wasn't an area known for large amounts of food. Perhaps, she was lost. He wondered if it was nearing three days since she had been in the shadowy darkness. It was more likely that she was already Light Blinded. There were a few of the Light Blinded who dwelled in the Skotad mountains, but no one had heard of any new ones for quite some time.

Toler felt a bit torn. If he shot her, he could carry her back to the mountain so that his Tribe could question her. For some selfish reason, he felt like he wanted to question her first. Perhaps, it was to understand why she was there. More than anything, he wanted to get a closer look at her odd tuft of blue hair.

Either way, it's not like she's dangerous… She's way too clumsy and loud…

"Or maybe it's a trap," he muttered softly to himself.

Erring on the side of caution, Toler snuck around the natural encampment with his arrow trained upon her at all times. He was immensely skilled at stealth although he was only eighteen years old. He had surpassed the greatest warriors in his Tribe.

Still, despite his expertise, he noticed that the Photak girl's body stiffened. He knew he had been made. Adapting his strategy, he immediately called out.

"Don't move, Photak! My arrow will puncture your flesh before you could reach for your bow."

He heard a little sigh. She must have calculated the distance to it herself, and she seemed to acknowledge that he was right.

"Come out from under there!" Toler commanded. "Slowly..."

He saw her lean body shift as he had instructed. She rolled out from under the canopy with her back facing him. Toler was a little thrown off by how calm she seemed and how even her breathing was. Something was not right. She didn't seem afraid. He wanted to see her face.

"Turn around, Photak!"

Slowly, she turned to face him, raising her head last.

Toler gasped. She was the most unusual girl he had ever seen... and she was beguilingly beautiful. He immediately searched her skin for her origins. A sense of terror struck him as he looked over any unconcealed skin she had. How was it possible?

She is... unmarked?!

She seemed to initially mirror his shock before concealing it with a cold stare. Her iridescent eyes narrowed as they rested upon the tip of his arrow.

"What… are you…?" Toler stammered.

A sly grin crept up one side of her face. Suddenly, she spun into the air in a pure Skotad attack filled with more power than Toler had ever seen. Shock ripped through him.

It's a TRA—

The world went black.

***

Yara stood over the Skotad, dagger held tightly. She had knocked him unconscious with its blunt end. She stared at him, genuinely perplexed at his appearance. It was her first time seeing a Skotad. She had expected silvery-white hair and pale skin. She even knew of their vividly blue eyes. This, however, was nothing like she had imagined.

Yara willed herself to focus and looked around for something with which to tie him. She found some strong vines a short way off. She dragged his body to the trunk of a tree and wrapped the vines around him. Testing her strength on the binds, she gave a satisfied smile before perching herself on a nearby boulder. Her eyes ran over his face and body.

He's so… beautiful…

Yara hated herself for thinking it, but this was no ordinary beauty. His skin glistened in the Shadows, and his long, silky hair looked like it was softer than the most expensive furs. And his face… his face was what she would imagine the face of an angel of Sunstar would look like. It was perfect, ruggedly handsome, but also so…

Kind… he looks so kind…

She wondered how he could even be evil. Then, she reminded herself that he had been the one to initiate the attack. Still, she hadn't been very careful. Technically, he could have shot her, killed her, with his arrow. She felt her curiosity grow as to why he hadn't. For that reason, and that reason alone, she had struck him with a nonfatal blow.

Now, she didn't quite know what she would do with him once he awakened.

"You could have left me a little room to breathe, you know?"

Yara jumped, startled that he was awake already. She shot him a glare.

"You have some nerve being so cheeky, especially as you're the one tied to a tree," she retorted.

"Perhaps, it's because my tribesmen are close by."

Yara felt her heartstar skip a beat, but she refused to let herself show it. Plus, she figured if that were true, he wouldn't want them to lose the element of surprise. He was trying to intimidate her.

"Well, let them come then... There are more vines and more trees all around..."

The Skotad seemed to assess her a little. Then, he changed his approach.

"I could have killed you, you know..."

It was effective. Yara couldn't help but feel a tinge of uncertainty. She had been taught that Skotads killed without hesitation. She had to admit to herself that the events over the past couple of days made her less confident in what she had been taught. Now, the Skotad seemed to have a reason he didn't kill her. She decided, given that he was tied to a tree, she had nothing to lose.

She jumped off the boulder and walked over to the tree. Lowering herself to his level, she faced him directly looking straight into his blue Skotad eyes.

"So... why didn't you?"

The Skotad smiled, and Yara felt her heartstar warm a little. She mentally scolded herself for it, remembering that he was still very much an enemy.

"Because I am not a senselessly violent Photak," he responded, eyes narrowing.

Yara balked at him and then responded with anger.

"We were never the senselessly violent ones! You Skotads have always been jealous of our ability to walk in Sunstar's light. You hated that we are the chosen ones! And you killed us for it. You killed our warriors, our gatherers, our children—"

The Skotad began to laugh. He laughed so hard that Yara wished she had just killed him in the first place. She felt infuriated. Eventually, as he seemed satisfied to see how upset she was getting, he settled down.

"So..." he said smiling, "unmarked though you might be, you are a Photak then? You must be, if you also believe the lies they have been telling their people for generations..."

Yara's mouth opened to respond, but nothing came out. She realized she had been baited. Still, she couldn't deny that there had indeed been lies... probably more than she even knew. She pressed her lips together, flew up, and knocked him out again.

That was enough for now... it was enough.

***

Toler opened his eyes slowly and peered through them. The pain in his head throbbed in pulsing waves. He winced. This Photak girl was a strong one… strong, and impressive. He had never been taken by anyone before. Not even by the best warriors of the mountains. A part of him wanted to rationalize it. He wanted to believe it was because he had never seen anyone who looked like her before. An unmarked, blue-haired girl.

But… how does she know how to fight like that…?

His head pounded the more he thought about it. It didn't make sense… not unless she was some kind of…

Photak weapon?!

If that were the case, then he knew his people were in grave danger.

Toler looked around for the Photak. She wasn't there. He searched for any signs of where she could have gone. His eyes narrowed as he saw broken twigs heading away from the where he had last seen her. He cursed himself. He was stuck to a tree, and no one knew where he was. It could be days before another Skotad came this way, if at all…

The low-lying canopy was Toler's secret hideout. He would go there whenever he needed time and space to clear his mind. The Photak girl had been the first person he had ever come across in this part of the Greens. It was known to be low in sustenance. He assumed that her presence there possibly meant that she too wanted to get away as much as he did. The question was,

What, or whom, is she running from?

He thought about what he did know. He knew based on her appearance that she was around his age. He knew that her being able to see so well meant she had been Light Blinded for some time. He also knew this based on how calm she seemed to be about the darkness. He knew that she was a very skilled warrior, despite his initial impression.

He knew she didn't like to be teased.

Toler smiled with a small chuckle at how aggravated she had become. As much as his head was killing him with pain, he thought her rage to be a little endearing. He had never met a girl who could knock out a warrior… twice!

"Well, you look pleased with yourself," she called out as she walked towards him.

It was Toler's turn to jump.

"I was assessing your many endearing qualities. I'll add stealthy to the list," Toler responded grinning.

He had to admit, he felt a bit relieved that she had come back. Being stuck to a tree indefinitely wasn't how he had planned to spend the next few days.

She walked over to him and placed her pouch by his lips.

"Drink."

He regarded the pouch suspiciously but then

reminded himself that she could kill him at any time.

"In case this is deadly poison and therefore our last moments together, my name is Toler. I hope that name will haunt you for the rest of your life."

She huffed and shoved the pouch closer. He placed his lips over the pouch's opening and drank deeply. It was sapjuice. After he had his fill, he gazed at her. For once, a more serious look came to his face.

"Why are you helping me, Photak, and why haven't you killed me yet? Isn't that all you people know how to do? Plunge and plunder?"

She looked at him and gave a small, controlled smile.

"Well, I can't have you die of thirst before I torture you for information," she said with a sugary tone.

Toler laughed heartily even though a small part of him wondered if she was serious.

"You won't be able to get that information if you keep knocking me out! Let's make a deal. I'll talk with you a little if you stop bashing me on the head… and also if you tell me your name, Photak."

She seemed to consider whether it would make a difference if he knew her name. After a few seconds, she looked him in his eyes, tilting her head. Her next words left Toler completely baffled.

"I can't make any promises regarding your head. But it's Yara. And for the record, I never said that I was a Photak."

Chapter Eleven

Yara had to admit to herself that there was something about Toler's reaction that was... different. It enthralled her. Unlike the usual fear it struck in everyone else's eyes, Toler's burned with spirited curiosity. Even more than that, there was something that intrigued her about facing her new reality out loud. She wasn't a Photak. She didn't even know what she was. Somehow, for the first time in her life, she just felt...

Free…

Toler seemed to be deep in thought as he slowly trailed his eyes over her. He appeared to be probing for any hint that could clue him in on what she meant. She felt the corner of her lips tugging but resisted the urge to smile. She didn't know why, but she enjoyed seeing him trying to resist her lure. She also enjoyed seeing him fail at it.

"Okay, not-a-Photak, you have my attention."

"Mmmm… except, I have nothing more to say."

Toler screwed his face a little. It was clear he was unaccustomed to being at such a disadvantage. Yara couldn't blame him—she would hate it if she was in his shoes. She sighed, feeling a little guilty about his captivity.

"Look, Toler, its semi-clear to me that we aren't trying to kill each other. So, it's my turn to make a deal. You answer a few questions and tell me what you think you know about the Photaks… and

I'll set you free. We will both go our separate ways."

Toler grinned widely.

"Photaks aren't usually ready to hear the truth... but seeing as you're not a Photak, perhaps you will be the exception, not-a-Photak."

"You know, I did tell you my name..."

"Yes, but you also said you might not be a Photak... and I KNOW you aren't a Skotad. Wouldn't you be more focused on that if you were me?"

Yara huffed. She already found discourse with Toler to be exhausting. No one talked that much, or that cheekily, back in the village.

No one talked that much... to me...

It was a strange feeling that followed her realization. She couldn't figure out why he didn't seem more afraid of her.

Perhaps, he has seen scarier things...

Toler seemed to notice the shift in her mood. His voice softened.

"Yara... I really do have to ask... what... who

are you?"

Yara twisted her head and considered him.

"I'm the one who's asking the questions here. So… deal or no deal?"

"Hmm. Deal."

***

For the next couple of hours, Yara sat facing Toler and listening to him. It hadn't taken more than a couple of questions before he began chattering away on his own. He even seemed to forget that he was tied to a tree. At first, she felt cautious about his openness. After a while, though, her curiosity got the better of her. She settled in, and soon she got lost in his stories.

The narratives were similar to that of the Photaks, but Skotads, he claimed, were a peaceful and loving people. His account framed the Photaks as the antagonists. Their version of the history of the planet hadn't been anything like what she had been told before.

"Our mutual ancestors, many millennia ago, never intended for our Tribes to be at war," he had said, "but the Photaks were jealous of our relationship with our ancestors. Back then, when there were day and night, our ancestors would spend the nights teaching us their ways, and the days they would spend worshipping Sunstar and resting.

"The Photaks were never exposed to these intimate teachings. They were envious. They felt it was unjust. When the planet was attacked, our ancestors were annihilated. But somehow the weapon used to damage Mira's core, and kill them, was not able to kill the Photaks or the Skotads. We all survived... but Mira had stopped giving us day and night.

"The Photaks took advantage of the ever-present light and began to hunt and murder us. They wanted the knowledge of the ancestors and the language of the markings for themselves. We retreated to the mountains, where we have lived ever since. The Photaks began to teach every generation that followed that the Skotads were their enemy."

"But how do you even know that any of this is true?" Yara had asked. "Perhaps, the Skotads also taught lies to their generations."

"Because of the markings and what they say. We can read the markings. So, while your Elders kept the knowledge of the markings and their Truth away from your Tribe, our Elders insisted each Skotad generation be taught... just as our ancestors taught us."

"You can read the markings?! Even the symbols on the trees?" Yara had balked.

"Yes," Toler had replied proudly, "and I can teach you, if you want."

As Toler continued his stories, Yara felt excited for the first time in her life. The more she listened, the more she learned about their beliefs and customs, their children, and their way of living. It seemed like a fairytale, so dissimilar to her village and her upbringing. The one thing that was very much alike, though, was Toler's love for his parents and their love for him and each other. His father, like him, was a warrior, and his mother was a Tribe teacher. Toler seemed so proud when he spoke about them, especially about his father's nobility and bravery.

"Once when my father had gone scouting in the Greens, maybe around a decade ago," he continued, "he came across a Photak warrior and what looked like an Elder attacking one of their own from behind. A poor, defenseless food-gatherer. My father shot the warrior, and the Elder ran off. My father tried to revive her, but her wounds were severe... He knew she would die, but he still carried her close to where the warriors patrolled... as close to the edge of the Greens as he could risk. He was so broken about it... not just because he had been forced to kill but also because he felt like the Photaks were truly lost now... that despite living in the light, they would never see the light of their own ways…”

Yara felt her heartstar pounding so hard that she was sure Toler could hear it. She stared at him wide-eyed, mouth slightly open.

“Uh… are you okay? I’m sorry I can get a little carried away sharing—”

Yara jumped up and walked past him, disappearing from his sight. Pulling out her dagger, she swiped her hand down the vines at the back of the tree.

“You’re freeing me…?” Toler asked suspiciously as he loosened himself and rubbed the sore parts of his arms. “I talk too much, don’t I?”

“Yes, I’m freeing you. And, yes, you talk too much. But you held up your side of the deal. So, now we can both go our separate ways,” Yara stated stoically as she walked back to the low canopy and began to gather her things.

“But, where are you going to go…?”

"I'm hungry. And I'm done babysitting you."

Toler let out an exaggerated gasp.

"But you did tie me to a tree… Babysitting me was only fair," he replied smugly.

Yara rolled her eyes.

"Goodbye, Toler!" she called out as she began to walk away.

"Wait! I know a great place where food is abundant, not too far from here… but you won't find it without me…"

Yara paused mid-step. She turned to face him, eyes narrowed.

"Or I could just tie you back to the tree and bash your head in until you tell me, Skotad!"

"Oh, so we're back to Skotad and not-a-Photak again? Come onnnn… what do you have to lose? Plus, I can teach you what a few of the markings mean along the way…"

Yara's stomach grumbled loudly in response, further enabling an annoying, hooting Toler. What she was savagely hungry for, however, was the knowledge of the markings. There was no winning against either one of her appetites. Yara's shoulders dropped as she let out a heavy sigh.

This is such a bad idea…

***

Toler strolled alongside Yara and found himself staring at her as he did. She didn't seem to notice it much. He could tell she was engrossed by all the sights and sounds of the Greens, and by her newfound knowledge.

Or perhaps, she is just accustomed to people staring at her… for her entire life…

Toler wanted to ask her about it, but he didn't want to interrupt her childlike awe. He had been surprised at her almost immediate change in mood when he began to explain the markings around them.

"There it is again! That one!" she exclaimed with a smile, interrupting his thoughts.

She pointed her finger towards a large tree trunk. She had learned that the wooden pendant she had fashioned out of a Saptree's markings when she was younger had been the symbol of Sunstar. It was two curves, with their lines crossing like an arced X, each curve perfectly mirrored. When he told her, she seemed to have an array of emotions before she smiled to herself. Her eyes had gleamed as she had reached up to touch her pendant. Toler didn't know why but seeing her happy made him feel like she had never been happy before.

"Yara… where did you come from?"

Yara's smile instantly vanished, and Toler felt a small surge of regret.

"If you don't want to talk about it, it's okay. I know I can be very inquisitive. OH! We're here!"

Yara's pensive expression changed to relief as she surveyed the hidden bounty of Saptrees, and mushrooms of every kind, in a small pocket of the Greens. She ran to a Saptree and gently slit its trunk, pressing her mouth against it as she drank deeply. Toler laughed with amusement. He pulled out his hidden dagger. Yara eyed it closely, face still pressed into the soft trunk. He slivered into the trunk with swift, habitual precision, allowing a halved funnel to be drawn out from the tree.

"So, you don't have to look as ridiculous as you do squashing your face like that..."

Yara glared at him. Then, she squished her face into the trunk even more. Toler laughed so heartily that Yara felt herself beginning to giggle. The giggle grew into a full-on laugh, and they both couldn't stop for a full minute. Toler felt her laugh was the most delightful thing he had ever heard. By the time they had their fill of laughter, they settled into the mushroom patch and leisurely picked and ate.

Toler lay back, hands on his full stomach, and twisted his head to look at Yara.

"You aren't used to laughing, are you?"

She looked at him with a pensive expression.

"There wasn't much to laugh about in the village," she replied softly.

"You stop smiling every time I ask you about your past. I know that Light Blindness can be tough at first, but it does get easier over time. I know a few Photaks who lead very normal, happy lives, but they told me the transition was hard when they first left the rays of Sunstar behind."

"Light Blindness...?" Yara responded, brows furrowed.

"Yes... How long have you been able to see in the Shadows...?"

Yara stared at him and looked down.

"It's been a while, I guess... But... wait, the Photaks told you this?!"

"Yes, a few of them live in the mountains too—"

"Live like Skotads?!"

"Yes... Yara," Toler said with a touch of

irritation, “where else do you expect them to live when they can’t withstand Sunstar’s light anymore?”

“I guess, I never really thought about it…”

“Yes, because all you’ve ever thought was that Skotads were evil, came from evil, and only did evil things, right? Just like your honest and upright Photak Elders taught you?”

Toler sat up. He didn’t know why, but he was on the edge of his patience. He didn’t like the way she seemed to despise the Skotads even after all he had told her. Yara balked at him, and a sad expression came over her face. He lay back down in frustration.

Then, finally, she spoke.

“I don’t know where I come from… or what I am…”

Toler slowly rose and rested back on his elbows.

“What do you mean… Who were your parents…?”

"I don't know. No one does. My Tribe mother found me in the Greens as a baby."

Toler's eyes widened. Yara shifted uncomfortably at his stares and then gave him a half smile.

"They thought I was a Skotad weapon for quite some time… except for my loving parents, of course… and one or two others… As for everyone else, I'm not quite sure if they ever stopped thinking it…"

"What a compliment!" Toler joked, returning quickly to his jovial manner. It didn't take much for him to center himself.

"Was it because of how you fight?"

Yara looked at him, surprised.

"Well, that's a part of it, yes, but… do I really fight like a Skotad?"

Toler looked away while he tried to find the words to explain it.

"Well… not exactly. It's different but still

has the same foundational style… You're actually quite impressive!"

Yara beamed.

Then, both she and Toler stiffened. Before she could say a word, an arrow cut through the air and plunged straight into Toler's chest.

Chapter Twelve

"NO!"

Yara rushed to Toler's side. He was unconscious, but the arrow was on the opposite side of his heartstar. She thanked Sunstar, and then felt her pores rising. She slashed out her daggers. She could hear the attacker running towards them, and she could feel the fire building within her. As he broke into the clearing, Yara spun into the air to deal her deathblow.

"YARA!"

She could feel her heartstar stop in her daggered descent towards—

Kristos?!

She barely managed to divert the cut of her blades as she landed facing him. His eyes were squeezed shut, almost as if he had been expecting to die. Slowly, he opened them and peered at her.

"Yara… you're okay…"

He grabbed her and embraced her. Tightly.

Yara's thoughts raced. Kristos was here. He came to find her. But Toler… Toler needed help. She pushed Kristos back and grabbed his shoulders, looking pleadingly into his eyes. He squinted at her, clearly affected by the Blurry.

"We need to help him!"

"What…? Help who?!"

"Toler. We need to help him. He was kind to me. And his father—"

Yara's voice broke as tears filled her eyes.

"His father saved my mother from Malek's attack..."

Kristos' brows furrowed as his face filled with rage. He stumbled back flabbergasted, pushing her away.

"Help him... HELP HIM?! I thought he was holding you captive! But you want to HELP HIM? You want to help a SKOTAD?! No... NO! I thought there was no way you could be what they said you were! I came all this way to find out THEY WERE RIGHT?! You're in league with the SKOTADS?!"

Yara couldn't control her tears any longer. They streamed down her face in torrents. This wasn't the Kristos she knew. The Kristos she knew would believe her, believe in her. This wasn't him.

"No, Kristos, please. No! You know that's not true... You know it's not! Didn't... didn't my parents tell you...? Didn't they tell you what I discovered?! I was there when you spoke to Pekone... Malek was hiding in the shadows of Pekone's dwelling. He came out after you left, and I heard them talking about what they had done. Kristos... Kristos, you have to believe me!"

Kristos began to pace back and forth, holding his head between his bent arms.

"Yes, Yara, your parents told me. In fact, they told everyone. They told everyone what you accused a respected Elder of doing. Then, your father thought it wise to attack Elder Malek..."

Yara's heartstar felt like it had stopped beating. As Kristos slowed his pacing, she felt like she couldn't breathe. Her father... attacked an Elder... that could only mean...

"Kristos, what happened to my father...?"

Kristos looked down, unable to speak.

"KRISTOS, WHAT HAPPENED TO MY—"

"He's dead, Yara... He was executed a few hours after your letter was discovered... for attacking an Elder and for treason... and your mother is soon to be on trial... That's why I had to come to find you..."

Yara felt the world beginning to spin. Her stomach turned, and her body shook uncontrollably. As her legs weakened, she fell on her hands and knees. She bent over, shoulders heaving, and let out a traumatic cry. She cried for her father, for her part in his death, for her entire life.

Kristos knelt next to her and hugged her as best he could. She sobbed into him for a long time until she felt herself becoming numb. As her sobs turned into sniffles, Yara melted into the comfort of Kristos' arms. She had thought she would never see him again. Now, she couldn't imagine enduring this without him. Despite everything, she knew he loved her enough to risk his life...

And find me... in the Greens...

Yara glanced up and looked around, wiping her eyes and face. Slowly, she lifted her body and knelt facing Kristos, her face contorted in confusion.

"Kristos... how did you find me... and...

where is your Guiding Thread…? It couldn't have been easy finding me here… and it won't be easy finding your way back to the village without it when you have the Blurry… Though… actually… I'm much further away than just one mile… So, how did you—"

Yara felt a sharp pain cut through the side of her neck. As a massive dose of Sleeper entered her body, she looked at Kristos in aggrieved horror. The effect was immediate, surging ten times stronger than the inner fight's dosage.

"I'm sorry, Yara… I wish there were another way… but I can't lose my father too…"

Everything went black.

***

Toler slowly regained consciousness and felt the need to groan. His instincts told him otherwise. He silenced himself before it escaped his lips. He could hear the Photak warriors close to him, and there were lots of them. He opened his eyes slightly. He was still in the same place in the Greens. He shut them back quickly as he heard voices nearing where he lay.

"Well done, Kristos!" he heard one say.

"Indeed, the Elders will be proud. And so will Chief Lamad. Sunstar will honor your sacrifice today in capturing the blue-haired abomination," another one said.

"And you witnessed your first Skotad kill! Even though you could barely see it with the Blurry. But don't worry, it gets better over time. You're lucky she didn't realize right away that you were tricking her. If she wasn't so concerned about saving the nasty Skotad, she might have realized there was no way you could have shot him. Not with the Blurry. And we might not have been able to run out in time to save you from her wrath."

As they proudly recounted their attack on him, Toler willed himself to be as still as possible.

He could feel the glances in his direction. He felt helpless.

"She was distracted by the news of her father's death... and I don't blame her. I... I just can't believe she wanted me to save the Skotad... I can't believe it's all... true..." he heard a new voice say.

Toler felt a moment of gratitude that Yara had even tried to save him. His instincts had told him she was a good person. He was glad to know he was right. He noted to himself that the new voice sounded quite unlike the others. It sounded distraught. He assumed it was the "Kristos" whom they were congratulating.

"We told you she was consorting with him. You badly wanted to believe that she was being held against her will. Is this now proof enough for you? She is a Skotad weapon of some kind, and she needs to be interrogated as such!"

"She told me that the Skotad's father was

the one who saved her mother from Elder Malek... when Lana was attacked years ago in the Greens. I mean, I know the entire story is a lie, but what if they are the ones who have been lying to her... What if they had been turning her against us all along...? Maybe that's why she wanted to save him. He probably made her feel like she owes him..."

Toler felt confusion fill his thoughts as he listened to Kristos. Then, it all came back to him.

The Photak my father saved in the Greens... it was Yara's adopted mother... and... she lived!!!

"It doesn't matter now, Kristos. We all know it's a complete fabrication. And now that her father has been executed, her mother will stand trial for bringing this abomination into our village and risking all of our lives. And the abomination will be questioned. She will tell us all we need to know, by any means necessary. It's a pity she can survive in Sunstar's light... but Pekone has an even greater instrument prepped for her interrogation."

The Photaks around snickered maliciously. Then, they began to pack up their things. From the sound of it, their packing included an unconscious Yara. Within moments, they called to each other to move out.

When Toler was sure no one was there anymore, he opened his eyes and looked around. Convinced he was safe, he pushed himself up, panting as the groan finally escaped his lips. He dragged himself to a nearby Saptree and leaned on its trunk. Taking a deep breath, he clasped his hands around the Photak arrow and pulled it out quickly.

"Aaaarrrrrhhhhhhh!" he cried out in agony.

When the flash of intense pain subsided a little, he reached into his pocket and pulled out a brown packet of mirrored balm. He opened it and winced as he dabbed it deep into the puncture. The wound wasn't very deep, probably because the shot was taken at such a distance. The Photaks would have stayed far beyond the reach of his ears.

He pushed himself up and leaned back against the tree. As he drank from the Saptree to rejuvenate himself, his eyes fell on the marking of Sunstar on its trunk. He touched it lightly.

Toler sighed. He knew that what he was about to do would risk over a decade of Skotad research and secrets. He reached for the packet again. He squeezed out even more mirrored balm and began dabbing it all over his face, head, arms, hands, legs, and body. He didn't stop until he was completely covered in it. The balm glistened as it soaked into his skin, causing sparks of pain everywhere it touched.

He leaned against the tree, breathing heavily.

"Okay, Yara… I'm coming to get you…"

***

Yara felt herself sinking into depths way within herself. Around her, she heard the taunts of the Tribe's voices slashing into her like daggers and then disappearing.

"Blue-haired abomination!"

"You're no Photak."

"Weapon!"

"She doesn't deserve to live!"

"She's a Skotad."

"Cage her!"

"Kill her."

"KILL HER!"

Yara tried to scream, but nothing came out. She had no voice… she had no strength. She had nothing. She was no one. She had no place in this world. Her birth parents never claimed her. They knew keeping her would be a mistake. They weren't wrong. She had killed her Tribe father. She left the letter that caused his death. She should have never said anything. She deserved to die. She hated Malek. She hated the Elders. She hated herself…

"Yara..."

It seemed fainter than usual, at first... but she heard it again, from the depths within her.

"Yara..."

"Who... who are you...?"

"You need to arise, Yara. You must arise now!"

"I... I can't. I'm too weak. They used the Sleeper on me... The dose is too strong... I keep fighting it... but I'm losing... I can barely stop myself from sinking deeper into it..."

"You are powerful enough to triumph over this... but your power is not in the fight. It's in your surrender."

"What... what power...? I have no power..."

"You are only as powerful as you allow yourself to believe... Surrender, Yara... surrender and ARISE!"

As a massive wave of the Sleeper surged through her, Yara felt herself being pulled by its force. She still tried to fight it but felt herself lose stamina the more she struggled. She used the last of her strength to make one final desperate push against it. It responded with a pulse that obliterated the last of her willpower. Failing, she gave up. She surrendered and fell straight into the Sleeper's wave.

"YaraStar... do you know who you are?"

It was here. Energy. Dangerous, powerful energy. It was back. Crackling through the Sleeper with intense attacks.

"YaraStar... I know who you are."

Everything stopped. Then, every piece of her skin began to burn with heat. It was coming from within her, burning away all of the drug in her blood. Burning away the weakness. Burning everything. As it burned, it also began to release her. As her awareness came back, Yara's eyelids felt heavy. Slowly, she allowed a glimmer of light into them as she peeked through. She had somehow regained consciousness.

"Arise, Yara!"

Yara's body jumped involuntarily at the now-audible voice. Startled, she mentally shook herself. She could no longer tell the difference between her dream world and the real one. Perhaps there was none. Still, she knew within herself that the voice wasn't imaginary. She knew, because she was not supposed to be awake yet. It was impossible with the dosage she had felt. The voice had brought her back.

She glanced around trying to figure out where she was. Soon, the environment registered. She had snuck in there with Kristos once. It was one of the cells they used to keep Skotads for the extraction of information before their execution.

Kristos...

Yara felt a stab of anguish. The Sleeper. Kristos was the one who had used the Sleeper on her. The memory of what happened suddenly rushed back to her. His betrayal burned through her. She was here because of him. She needed to find her mother, and she needed to get them both out of the village. She looked around her, searching for anything she could use to pick the lock of the bars that stood in the way of her freedom. They wouldn't be expecting her to be awake this soon. It was the perfect time.

Suddenly, she heard the sound of footsteps coming down from the upper keep. Her heartstar sank. She was too late.

Chapter Thirteen

Yara stilled herself and closed her eyes.

Perhaps, if the person thought she was still under the effects of the Sleeper, she would be left alone again. She needed time to make a plan, and she needed space to do it. As she heard the footsteps softly nearing her cell, she did her best to even her breathing. She could feel her eyelids anxiously fluttering against her strong will. She could only hope the person would think she was dreaming.

The person seemed to pause, and for the next few moments, there was only silence. Then, the unbelievable happened.

"Yaaarrraaa..."

A soft whisper cut through the air. It couldn't be. Yara flew up and turned to face a most welcome sight.

"Mila!" Yara exclaimed.

"SHHHHHHHhhhhhhhh!"

"I'm sorry," Yara whispered back, thoughts racing. "Mila, what are you doing here? How did you find me? How did you even get in the main keep?"

Mila grinned triumphantly.

"I have my ways," she giggled with pride.

"For once, your sneaking has paid off, hasn't it MilaStar? Okay, give me the report, young warrior."

"Well, they didn't think you'd be awake for a while. They're pretty silly, thinking you're weak like that. I knew better, so when they went to their meeting, I snuck in."

"Mila, how many guards did you have to sneak past?"

"Only four. And they were all talking. You've caused a big stir, Yara... They're saying you're a..."

Mila looked down, brows furrowed.

"That I'm a Skotad?"

Mila nodded and peered up at Yara through the cell bars. Then, she earnestly continued, "But I told you... even if you are a Skotad... I'd still think you're the best. And I do, Yara. But... I'm scared for you. I think they want to hurt you..."

Mila broke into soft weeping, covering her face with her hands. Yara's expression saddened. She sat on the floor so she could face Mila.

"Well... I don't know what I am just yet... but I did meet a Skotad... and from the way he looked, I'm not that either."

Mila looked up from her fingered cocoon.

"Well, you need to tell them! You need to tell them, so they don't hurt you... or worse... especially after what they did to your..."

Mila fell silent, unable to finish, her eyes watering again.

Yara felt an overwhelming pang of pain rip through her. She hadn't begun to process the loss of her Tribe father. It was too hard to believe. Even worse, all executions were done publicly, and all Photaks were required to bear witness... including her Tribe mother, and even little Mila. Yara felt her anger rise. Her cold, hot rage against Elder Malek and his treachery felt unbearable.

"Listen, Mila. I have already wrongfully lost my father. I need to save my mother. The fact that they have me here in this cell means that her trial is simply obligatory. They have already decided she is guilty... guilty of simply rescuing me from the Greens as a baby and raising me. I can't let them kill her. I can't... I can't lose her too."

Mila's lips tightened as she nodded with determination.

"We are going to save her, Yara."

"No, not we—I will save her. No, no, don't protest, Mila. I'm serious this time. I won't be able to forgive myself if anything ever happens to you too. I don't want you to risk any more than you already have. We just need to find me a way out of this cell and back to the Greens. I will do the rest. Okay?"

"Sigh. Okay, Yara. What should I do?"

"Pass me something that I can use to pick this lock. In the meantime, I want you to do what you do best, young warrior—sneak around and scout. I will need to find a way that isn't heavily guarded out of the village. Can you do that for me, Mila?"

"Yes! I can!"

"Good. Have you seen where they are keeping my mother?"

"Yes... they have her bound by the stones. They have had her there since they killed... your father. She has to stay there until her trial. It starts in a couple of hours—around the time they think you will be awake."

"How many guards did they post there?"

"Only two... then they all went to Pekone's dwelling for their meeting. All the Elders, and the Chief. The Chief looks sad. They said that if Kristos hadn't brought you back, they would have sent Chief Lamad to Light Banishment. They blame the Chief for everything. They said he was the one who broke the Elders' tied-vote that let you stay when you were a baby. Kristos was trying to save him, so he had to come to get you."

Yara gasped. As Mila searched around for broken blades to pick the lock, Yara remembered the impossible position in which the Elders had put Kristos. Her heartstar sank at the choice she knew he had been forced to make.

"Will this work?" Mila asked, interrupting Yara's thoughts.

"Yes, I think so. Let me see..."

As Yara examined the blade and tried fitting it into the lock, Mila asked her about the Greens and her journey there. Yara briefly told her all she had seen and the beauty of the flora.

"And... the Skotad? What did he look like?"

Yara felt a sense of sadness. She knew that Toler couldn't have survived the arrow wound on his own. She also knew it was only because of her that he had been attacked.

She sighed.

"Well... he's dead now... but he was kind to me... I don't know if all Skotads are like him, but if they are, then we have been wrong about them all along... the Photaks shot him straight in the chest because he was with me..."

"Yara... I think you're wrong. I think they would have killed him even if he was not with you..."

Yara huffed in response. Mila was growing up so much faster than she had realized. She reached out through the bars and tousled her red hair.

"When did you get so smart, little one?"

Mila grinned with pride.

"Always was! So... tell me before I go... what was the Skotad's name? And what do Skotads really look like?!"

"Toler... his name was Toler..."

***

As Toler neared the edge of the Greens surrounding the village, he could feel his heartstar pounding harder. He had been scouting for some time, trying to find a way in that wasn't heavily guarded. He had observed the general direction the Photak warriors came and went from, so he had an idea of where they could be holding Yara. Still, he did not know precisely where she would be or, even more importantly, how long he would be able to last in Sunstar's rays.

This is suchhhhhh a bad idea… stupid… stupid… stupid idea…

Toler sighed. He knew his father would be furious if he knew all that Toler was risking. He shook his head as a small smile came to his lips.

"I'm just following in your footsteps, father. You saved her mother… and now I must save her…" he muttered to himself.

As he crept towards the feathered trees lining the edge, Toler's eyes fell on what seemed to be an overgrown path through the shrubbery. It was so overgrown, in fact, that he was certain it had not been used in decades. Toler observed the line of light in front of him, along the edge of the Greens. He had tested the mirrored balm secretly before, but it had not been cleared for use. The Skotad Tribe wanted to leave the mountains and caves, and find places to dwell away from the Photaks and their love of war. This was their chance to do it. With the mirrored balm, they could finally travel through Sunstar's rays to find somewhere new to dwell.

Toler reached his hand out into the light. It felt warm, and a bit painful, but more tolerable than the last time he had attempted to test the mirrored balm. He grinned. Sunstar was definitely on his side. He could only hope it would last long enough for him to save Yara, primarily as he had already used all the balm.

He crept out to the feathered trees, looking around and listening for movement. He heard none. He proceeded along the edge until he was the shortest distance possible from the shrubbery. He took a deep breath, pulled out his dagger, and carefully made his way towards the small opening. It would be his first time entering a Photak village. He wasn't going to take any chances, even with the cover of the overgrowth.

As he reached the overgrown path, he bent down low and backed into it while searching the area again. Relieved that he couldn't see anyone, he pushed further in and turned around. His eyes widened, and he froze. There, right in front of him, was a small Photak girl. She was staring at him with wide, terrified eyes and had a tiny dagger.

Toler felt his heartstar panging in fear. His thoughts raced as they stared at each other, neither of them moving a muscle. He couldn't figure out how he hadn't heard her, but seeing how still she stayed seemed to explain why. The girl's eyes left his and began to trace his body. They paused on his chest, on his wound. Her little brows furrowed with concern, and all her fear seemed to vanish.

"You're hurt…" she whispered.

Toler, stunned at her bravery, stammered softly back in response.

"Well, you Photaks seem to enjoy sticking us with arrows…"

The girl gasped and looked at him with a strange sense of recognition.

"You're... Toler?"

Toler jolted unconsciously. His thoughts raced even more. He wondered if Yara had been tortured for information. He wondered if he was too late.

"How do you know that name, little one?"

She grinned slyly.

"If you tell me whether that's your name or not, I'll tell you how I found out," she replied cheekily.

Toler huffed, cracking a smile. She was a little Photak negotiator. He liked her already.

"Yes, little Photak. That is, indeed, my name. It's nice to meet you. And what's your name?"

A look of pure excitement filled her face.

"I'm Mila. I'm Yara's bestest friend. Yara thinks you died. She's going to be sooo happy that you didn't die. She said you were kind to her. Thank you for being kind to my YaraStar. She sent me on a mission to find a way out of the village for her that doesn't have guards. They're keeping her in a cell, and they think she is still under the Sleeper. But Yara is soooo strong, so she is already awake, and they don't know she is. I'm going to save her and her mother. Yara is picking the lock for the cell as we speak, and I'm going to report back to her on this path I found. She would be expecting me back with my report now. I'm a young warrior, you know?"

Toler's mouth opened with wonder at Mila's sudden burst of quick, quiet chatter.

"Well… you most certainly are, brave little warrior. And guess what? I'm here to save Yara too. You think maybe we can work together?"

Mila nodded enthusiastically, and then looked at him in confusion.

"But how… how did you get here? I thought Skotads couldn't walk in Sunstar's rays. Well, then again, I also thought Skotads were ugly monsters, but you are really cute… for a stupid boooooyyy! Yara didn't tell me that part…"

Toler chuckled a little.

"I'll be sure to complain that she should have told you how cute I am the next time I see her. And as for me in Sunstar's rays, this is only a temporary solution… and I don't know how long I have… so we will have to be quick about this rescue, okay?"

Mila gave a solemn nod.

"But first…" she said, pausing with her lips pursed, "you need a disguise. You look too pale, and your hair is too white. You would be spotted as easily as I saw you. I'm going to get you a swaddling cloth. I'll be back."

***

As Mila led Toler through hidden paths, his admiration for her grew. Although she was just a child, she was wise beyond her years. She taught him a little along the way about places to avoid and what she thought he should know. She spoke highly of Yara and how incredible she thought Yara was. She spoke about the Photaks' inner fight and how everything went wrong after that. She exuded loving admiration with every word. She seemed determined to save Yara. It was a stark contrast to the conversations he had overheard from the Photak warriors who shot him.

As they neared the end of the shrubbery, Mila pointed out the main keep. A mostly open area surrounded it, but there were still a few places to hide. Mila said it was the warriors' training ground. As Toler spotted a couple of guards standing by an elevated structure made of stone, he instinctively pulled the cloth closer around him. Mila pointed towards it.

"There, do you see her? That's Lana… Yara's Tribe mother. They have had her bound there since they killed Sorin… Yara's Tribe father. No one is allowed to speak to her… They haven't even given her sapjuice to drink."

As Toler squinted his eyes, he could see Lana's red hair waving slightly in the wind. Her head was lowered, and she seemed weak. This was the Photak woman his father had saved so many years ago. She had sacrificed so much for Yara.

Toler felt a pang of rage rise and fill him. Photaks were such a cruel people. He wondered how they could ever think they were Sunstar's chosen ones when they would hurt even their own in such gruesome ways.

A wave of burning hit Toler's skin. He knew he didn't have much time left. He turned towards Mila.

"Okay, let's save Yara, and then we'll save her mother. We will get them both out of here. But we need to do this quickly, Mila. I don't have much time left in Sunstar's rays."

Mila's eyes widened with concern as she nodded. He felt a sense of warmth that she seemed to care about his wellbeing. He took her hand into his. As he began to step out of the shrubbery, Mila grabbed his hand and yanked him back.

"Wait! There's Kristos. That's the Chief's son who brought Yara from the Greens."

Toler and Mila stared helplessly as Kristos made his way into the main keep where Yara was being held.

Chapter Fourteen

As Yara heard footsteps approaching, she felt a sense of relief. She hadn't been able to pick the lock with the broken dagger, and she needed Mila to find her something else to use. She knew she had maybe an hour again before they would wonder if she was awake. She needed to be far into the Greens with her Tribe mother by then. She got up and leaned on the bars as the footsteps reached the bottom of the stairs.

"Finally!" she exclaimed, and then gasped.

Kristos looked equally in shock.

"You're awake!"

"Well… I was wondering… when you would come to see me. Because I think you owe me an explanation…"

Kristos looked away with guilt, and Yara breathed with relief. He didn't seem to realize she had been expecting someone else.

"I'm sorry, Yara," he said softly. "They didn't give me any choice. They were going to banish my father and force Light Blindness upon him. He would never have been able to dwell in Sunstar again. And I would have lost him forever…"

"Well, I think there's always a choice," Yara stated coldly, "but I guess I understand. But now *my* father is dead, and my mother may be soon… and then me…"

Kristos hung his head. He seemed to be in agony. For the next few moments, the silence between them seemed to scream. Yara felt awkward. She had known Kristos for her entire life. He had been her friend. He had been the boy she loved. Now, it felt like there was a widening chasm between them. It was noble of him to want to save his father, but his decision to do that meant he knew she would be killed. She wondered how he could have ever said he loved her.

But he did come to see me…

"Kristos, if you thought I was still under the Sleeper, why are you here?"

"Elder Malek sent me to check on you…"

Yara's face contorted in anger at the name of the Elder. She felt even more than that. She felt hate. Pure, unadulterated hatred.

"So, you follow Malek now?!"

"I'm a Photak warrior now, Yara. I took an oath…"

"An oath to serve a man who tried to kill an innocent woman for taking me in as a baby?! And you think that's honorable?!!"

"He didn't do that, Yara! Whatever that Skotad bastard was telling you, they are all lies!!! And you are more gullible and stupid than I thought for even believing him. Who was he anyway?! Who was he to you, Yara?!"

Yara let out a sarcastic laugh.

"Oh, so you're my interrogator? What are you going to do if I don't tell you what you want to hear? Are you going to let them torture me, Kristos? Are *you* going to torture me?"

"Please, Yara... please... you just need to tell the truth. Tell them what you know. Tell them enough to save your life!"

"I AM TELLING THE TRUTH, KRISTOS! I heard Pekone and Malek with my own ears. I keep telling you, and you won't listen to me. I don't know how else to say what I saw or what I heard. I can tell you every word of your conversation with Pekone! What do I need to do to convince you?! Why don't you believe me?! It's ME, Kristos. It's me..."

Kristos looked at her with pained eyes.

"Then why were you with him, Yara... Why were you with a Skotad... and why did you want to save him?"

Yara felt helpless. She didn't know how she could even begin to tell Kristos that everything they had been taught was a lie... that the Skotads were good people. She knew if he didn't believe her about Malek, he wouldn't believe anything more.

"Does it even matter now? They killed him..."

Then, a strangely familiar, annoyingly cheeky voice called out.

"Well, they tried. But I'm not quite dead yet!"

***

"Toler! You're alive!"

Toler grinned, feeling warmed by Yara's happiness, while Kristos stared at him in speechless shock.

Then, Kristos ripped out his daggers and ran charging towards Toler. Toler jumped back, barely escaping the slashing blades.

"Not bad, Photak. How about you try that attack for real this time?"

Kristos spat as Toler pulled out his dagger and crouched in his fight stance.

"I should have slit your throat after they shot you, Skotad," Kristos said coldly.

"Kristos, please... I told you, Toler was kind to me. He isn't what you think he is."

"Yet somehow he is here... in our main keep... a Skotad... our lifelong enemy. How are you here, Skotad? Shouldn't you be dead from Sunstar's rays by now?"

Toler heard Yara gasp in reaction to the truth of Kristos' words. She looked at him, searching for an explanation.

"Or maybe," Kristos continued, "this is how

you were able to plant your Skotad weapon among us all this time…"

"Kristos…"

Toler could feel the pain in Yara's voice. For the first time, he realized that this was someone for whom she cared. He felt angry for her.

"Yara may be a lot of things… a lot of amazing, beautiful things… but she is neither a Skotad nor a Skotad weapon. She may not know where she comes from, but I, for one, am glad she exists."

Toler looked towards Yara and gave her a reassuring smile. Then, he looked back at Kristos with a fiery glare.

"And Yara," Toler continued, "just so you know… this Photak scum doesn't deserve you."

Kristos charged angrily at Toler. Toler spun into the air, and as Kristos passed under him, Toler drove the back of his dagger into Kristos' head. Kristos fell to the ground, unconscious.

Yara rushed as close as she could get to where Kristos fell.

"Soooo… should I kill him now or later?"

"NO! No… don't kill him…"

Toler lowered himself to face a concerned Yara.

"I was only joking, Yara…" he said softly. "We have only ever killed in self-defense, and even when it's justified, it is still not our way. The fact that you don't want him hurt after what he did tells me that it is not your way either…"

"You don't know what my ways are… Even I don't know what my ways are…"

"Perhaps, but what's more important is that we get you out of here. I don't have much time left. I will need to get back into the Shadows as soon as we get your mother."

"Wait… we?"

"Yes, I met your little warrior, Mila. She was the one who helped me find you. She is quite a smart little one, isn't she? She went to see how best we can free your mother. They have her bound by the stones."

Yara beamed.

"She's the bravest person I know, Toler, but we need to protect her. If they find out she helped me, I don't know what they would do to her..."

Toler nodded in solidarity.

"Let's get you out of there," he said.

"I've tried," Yara responded, holding up the broken blade.

Toler grinned. He reached towards Kristos' unconscious body and pulled the keys out of his pocket. Yara laughed when she saw them.

"How did you..." she started.

"Mila," they then said in unison, smiling.

Only she would have thought that Kristos might have had them. She would have sent Toler after him because of that lucky guess. She was such a smart, sneaky young'un.

Three key tries later, and Yara was finally free. As they made a quick plan for escape, they moved Kristos' body into the cell and locked it again. They couldn't risk him waking up and running off to warn the Elders and warriors. They had only one chance.

Yara turned to face Toler squarely, her expression inquisitive.

"Why are you risking your life for me?"

"It's nothing my father didn't do for your mother… right?" he responded with a grin. "I guess, risking our lives to save distressed Photak women, or in this case a not-a-Photak woman, runs in the family."

Yara balked at Toler, realizing he must have overheard a conversation about it. She was also clearly aggravated by the very notion that she needed to be saved. She fired a small glare at him, and then, her face grew serious.

"Let's do this."

***

As they snuck up the stairs, Yara listened out for any movement. Toler had told her the way he had used to get past the guards. If they were lucky, that way would still be clear. As they reached the main entrance to the cells, they looked in the direction of the passageways. There was no one there.

Yara breathed a sigh of relief and nodded at Toler. They snuck along the walls and through the labyrinth of passageways. They passed the storage room for weapons along the way. Yara found her weapons stashed there. She quickly suited up, and they continued on their way. It was the long path out, but it was also the safest. As they reached the foyer that stretched into the training grounds, Toler hesitated. He seemed to be eying the light that formed an edge along the entryway. He glanced at Yara and tried to muster a smile.

"It's going to hurt, isn't it?" Yara said softly, reaching her hand towards him in concern.

"I can handle it... we just need to be quick

about it, okay?"

Yara could tell he was trying to be strong for her. She worried for him, but she smiled confidently for the sake of his peace of mind.

Suddenly, they heard a commotion coming from the direction of the stones. There were shouts and a small scream. A scream from a little Photak girl.

"MILA!" Yara shouted in panic.

Without thinking, she raced towards the stones.

"Yara, no! STOP!" she heard Toler call after her, but she couldn't.

No… no… no. Not Mila. Please, don't let her be hurt. Please, Sunstar, please…

As Yara neared, she could see a group of warriors gathered around the stones. Then, she saw him. Elder Malek was holding Mila roughly by the back of her neck. Behind them, Lana lay weakly on the ground. Mila had a cup in her hands, clearly having brought sapjuice for Yara's mother. It would be for this that Malek would have little Mila disciplined… for kindness.

"Maaallleeeeekkkkkk!!!" Yara screamed out in anger.

Malek jumped, turning quickly towards the sound. As he saw her approaching, his eyes opened wide, and his jaw dropped. He began shouting at the warriors who had accompanied him. They all turned to face her and readied themselves for a fight.

Yara didn't care how many there were. She felt rage. She felt hate. She wanted Malek dead. She wanted to kill him herself. She slashed out her daggers and let out a guttural battle cry. She heard not just her voice but also Toler's. It was only then she realized that he had run out behind her. She felt strengthened by his presence.

They plunged into the line of Photak warriors in unison, each swinging into the air and flying back down in attack. One by one, they flattened warrior after warrior. With only two warriors left standing, they turned to launch their final attack.

"YARA! Are you sure you want to continue putting down my warriors?" Malek called out.

As Mila screamed again, Yara turned to see Malek holding a blade against her mother's throat.

"NO! WAIT!" she shouted. "Please, don't... PLEASE..."

Malek chuckled in response.

"If you want to save your mother, I'd advise you drop your weapons," he sneered.

Yara's body shook. She knew she had been defeated. As she gazed into her mother's desperate eyes, she felt her daggers slide out from her hands and land with a thud on the ground. She glanced towards Toler. He looked visibly in pain now. His time was up.

"I see Sunstar is finally getting to you, Skotad," Malek said with scorn. "Killing you by our blades will be a mercy you don't deserve. Soon, the rays will melt your flesh, and I want everyone to witness it. Tie him to the stones!"

Yara watched helplessly as the two warriors dragged Toler up the structure and bound him with ropes.

"You Photaks have a thing for tying us up, I see," Toler stammered, managing to give her a small wink.

Yara shook her head. Toler was about to experience the most painful death. She couldn't believe he was still cheeky about it.

"MILA!"

Everyone swung around to see Mila's mother hustling towards the stones. She was fuming. As she reached and saw Yara and Toler, she glared at Elder Malek.

"You said the blue-haired abomination would be dead by now. You promised us this. Yet, here she stands, and she is here with a Skotad! How are you protecting our Tribe? Why isn't she dead?!

Kill her!" May exclaimed.

Malek's eyes narrowed. He didn't like being criticized or ordered around.

"She will die once we have extracted the information we need from her," he replied coldly.

May huffed in seething disapproval, shaking her head.

"Mila! Come here now!" May shouted. When Mila was close enough, May grabbed her by her ears.

"I told you to stay away from the abomination! And her mother! Why are you even here?!"

As she pulled her away, Mila swung around with tears, looking at Yara. Yara gave her a small smile and nodded gratefully. They could hear May screaming at Mila all the way out the training grounds. Yara shook her head and looked coldly at Malek.

"Let my mother go, Malek. Let her go, and I'll tell you whatever you want to know."

Malek lowered his blade and smiled in the evilest of ways. He looked out in the direction of Pekone's dwelling. Yara turned to see all the warriors returning to the training grounds, heading in her direction. She glanced back at Toler. His skin was reddening, and he looked like he was about to scream out in pain.

Yara's heartstar sank. There was so much pain and sorrow caused by her existence. As the alarm sounded and the Photak warriors rushed to the stones, her heartstar beat faster and faster. Her Tribe mother's eyes pierced her with sadness. At this stage, Yara was ready to tell Malek anything he wanted to hear to save her. She would even claim she was a Skotad and that she had known all along.

As the warriors gathered around with hooting war cries, Yara looked pleadingly at Malek. Finally, he spoke.

"Yes, Yara, you are going to tell me everything you know. But first, let's make sure you don't get distracted trying to save anyone again."

Then, Malek plunged his blade straight into Lana's heartstar.

Chapter Fifteen

Yara's screams could be heard as far away as the dwellings. They rippled with agony from her tormented soul. She rushed to her Tribe mother's side, wailing and begging anyone to help. No one moved, and some of the warriors turned away. Behind her, Toler's skin had begun to melt. He could no longer hold in his anguish. His cries intertwined with hers. It was the sound of a haunting hell.

There was no day in Photak history quite

like this one. In many ways, there would be no other like it again. As her mother let out her final breath, dying in Yara's arms, something in her finally broke.

Yara heard a whisper on the wind.

"Your power is in your surrender..."

She slowly got up and turned to face a calm Malek. She eyed his blood-stained dagger. Then, she looked him intensely in his eyes and said, "I surrender."

***

Toler awoke to find himself on a vined stretcher in the Greens. He was certain he had died. He wondered if this was where Skotads went after death. As he tried to look around, searing pain blazed through his body with even the slightest shift.

Nope. Definitely not dead.

He closed his eyes and breathed gently until

the blistering pain eased. He tried to remember what had happened and how he got there. He had strange flashes of memories. The Photak village. Little Mila. Rescuing Yara from the cell. Attacking the warriors with her. Sunstar's rays beginning to penetrate his skin.

Everything else felt unclear. He knew the Elder had mercilessly killed Lana. And Yara was broken by it… she told Malek she surrendered. Then, the Photak warriors were… motionless. They were all standing and jeering, and then, in the blink of an eye, they all fell to the ground. Everyone, everywhere around them. And Yara… Yara was standing over them all. Malek's body lay in front of her. She stooped down staring at him with pure hate, and he at her, dagger in her hand. She looked like she was about to kill him when Toler screamed out in pain. Yara had rushed to his side.

Toler didn't remember anything that happened after that. He had lost consciousness from the pain. Now, he had no idea where in the Greens he was, and from what he could hear, there was no sign of Yara or anyone else around. He thought about the look of pure hatred on her face when she stood over Malek. He wondered if his burning agony hadn't interrupted her...

Would she have killed him? For revenge?

A part of Toler couldn't blame Yara if she had killed Malek, especially after what Malek had done to her Tribe mother. Still, it would have been an act of hate. That form of justice simply wasn't the Skotad way. They held fair trials if there were perpetrators, and judgments were always made with compassion.

Toler worried for Yara. She had been through more than anyone else he had ever known. She had experienced more pain than anyone ever should.

"Well, thank Sunstar, you're finally awake..." a soft voice called out as quiet footsteps pattered towards him.

Yara walked up with sapjuice in a makeshift

cup. She knelt by his side and observed the exposed areas of his skin and the wound in his chest, frowning.

"It is a little better with the crushed medicine I made from the roots of a few of the plants here, but it still looks so inflamed. And your chest is beginning to look infected. I need to find you help. I've searched for quite some time, but I can't seem to find the way to your people."

Toler observed Yara. She looked utterly worn out. She also looked like she had been crying for hours. He couldn't imagine her state of devastation. He didn't know how he would manage if both his parents had been killed.

As Yara continued to attend to his wound, pasting on the medicine she had made, Toler wondered how it was even possible for them to be there. He was confident they had lost. He was sure they would die. Yet, somehow…

"Yara, how did you defeat so many warriors?

And how did I get here? How far are we from your village?"

"I carried you... and don't worry, we're very far from the village. I headed north towards the mountains, in the general direction they told us that Skotads came from to enter the Greens... but the Greens stretch out for so very far."

"How many hours have I been unconscious? How long have you been carrying me?"

"Hours? Toler, it's been two days. I was so worried you wouldn't make it."

Toler felt horrified.

"Yara... you must be exhausted... thank you, thank you for saving my life..."

"I was only returning the favor," she responded with a small, sad smile.

"But how... how did they all fall... all of them, they were surrounding us, and then... I... I don't understand what happened..."

Yara looked away with deep sadness and fear.

"I don't know, Toler..."

***

In some ways, Yara wished that what she was telling Toler was a lie. At the same time, she wasn't sure she wanted to know the truth about what had happened back at the training grounds. She was scared of what she felt inside of her... of what she was and her origins. The irony was not lost on her—for the first time in her life, she was feeling what the Photak Tribe had felt about her all along.

Perhaps, they were right to be afraid of me...

She sighed. She felt exhausted physically and mentally. Whatever had powered through her, defeating the Photaks with a massive pulse of energy, had also drained her.

To make matters worse, emotionally, Yara was completely unhinged. The only thing that had kept her going was knowing that Toler's life was on the line. She refused to let him die, especially after all he had sacrificed to save her.

Yara couldn't believe the pain her life had caused to those around her. More than anything, she couldn't believe her parents were dead. It had crushed her until she couldn't breathe. Yara had tried to stay focused on getting Toler to safety. She had attempted to distract herself from her agony, but there were so many times that it seemed he wouldn't make it. The very thought that he could die only brought back the tidal waves of grief she felt for her mother and father. It hadn't been long before she lost all control, and her attempts to remain focused were obliterated.

Yara had spent the past two days broken, screaming to a silent Sunstar over and over again for an explanation. There had not been a moment she had not cried, and there had not been a minute that she didn't question why it had to happen to her loving parents.

What is it all for? Why do people have to suffer

because of me? Why does Sunstar allow this all to happen?! WHY DO YOU ALLOW THIS TO HAPPEN?!!!

In her darkest moments, coincidentally, Toler would suddenly groan. His groans were the only signs she had that he could regain consciousness. They also made her feel like her deep distress was hurting him even more. In those times, she did all she could to concentrate on finding him the herbs he needed, all through tear-filled eyes.

Grateful that he was finally awake, Yara gently raised Toler's head to help him drink. As he winced in pain, she considered the extent of his kindness. She couldn't understand why he would put himself through all of this for her. He didn't even know her. He had only just met her a few days ago. If she was honest, most of that time he had spent unconscious.

Yara had tried searching for the Skotads in all areas surrounding the north, but to no avail. She knew that if the Skotads were as similar to him as he had claimed, they would do anything they could to save his life. One time, she wondered what her life would have been like if she had been found by the Skotads instead…

At least, my mother and father would still be alive… I would never have known them, but at least they wouldn't have suffered and died because of me…

She felt guilty for thinking it, but she also knew she was right. Nothing about this was worth it to her. She wondered how the purpose of her Tribe parents' lives could have been to experience such painful deaths for choosing to love her. She continued to angrily question a still-silent Sunstar as to why her Tribe mother had been the one to find her.

More than any other feeling, she felt angry at herself. She hated all that she was, or perhaps all that she wasn't. She also hated Malek for what he had done. She had so badly wanted to kill Malek …

But Toler's life is worth far more than Malek's ever

will be... I need to save him...

She looked at Toler now with brows furrowed sorrowfully.

"We need to find your people, Toler," Yara said softly as she brushed a few strands of his silvery-white hair away from his eyes.

Toler stared intensely at her, seeming to consider what she said while weighing it against everything else. Eventually, he sighed.

"While all are welcome to the mountains, it is dangerous for a new person to arrive unannounced. The entrance is well-hidden and kept a secret. Anyone unexpected who approaches can be shot from a distance if word isn't sent ahead... because it can be perceived as an attack and Skotads can kill in self-defense," he said weakly. "However, it is pretty clear with my condition that I can't go ahead to announce you. Even worse, the way you are dressed closely resembles Photak warrior garb, and you don't look like anyone they would have ever seen… and you will have a very injured Skotad hostage with you… or so it will seem. I am worried that I won't get a chance to explain… that you won't get a chance…"

"I don't care, Toler… and surely once they recognize you, they will want to save your life. You're a warrior, and you're the son of a warrior, right?"

"Uhh… something like that…"

"Well, regardless, we're doing this, Toler. We are going to get you help. I will do my best to explain to you where we are now, and you will tell me where to go from here, okay?"

"Has anyone ever mentioned how stubborn you are?"

"I'd hurt you if you weren't already in so much pain," Yara shot back. "Listen up, now. This is the path I took."

As Yara explained to Toler how they got to where they were, she was relieved to find out that they weren't very far away from the Skotad territory. She had seen a couple of the landmarks that Toler spoke about along the way. She had chosen a route that she had felt guided to take, although she couldn't explain why she had.

Yara got them both more sapjuice and fed Toler mushrooms in preparation for the journey. As she packed up, she heard him whisper words of gratitude to Sunstar for her, asking for her protection. She pretended not to hear, feeling self-conscious and undeserving. She walked over to him when she was certain he was done with his prayerful murmurs. She observed the vines that she had wrapped to make his stretcher. She looked at him with concern.

"The entire time I was dragging you along, you were unconscious. Now that you're awake, every second of this is going to be torture for you. Are you sure you don't want me to leave you here and go get help?"

"No," Toler said firmly, "you stand a better chance with me there. I can take it, Yara. What I can't take is anything else happening to you..."

Yara sighed, looking away and shaking her head. While she knew he was right, he had already been through so much. The torture he would have to endure was unfathomable. She knew she would need to get him help quickly, and not just because of the difficult journey. The wound to his chest had not been treated properly, and he was starting to get a high fever. Time was of the essence.

As she raised the ends of the stretcher, she empathetically winced when she heard his gruff, pained breaths. She looked back, and he nodded. Then, she looked forward and willed herself not to react to what she knew was to come.

As she took off, Toler's guttural cries penetrated the Green's thick foliage. She could tell he was trying to muffle it with his hands. As they neared the third landmark, she knew the Skotads on guard would be faintly hearing his cries. She tried to stay alert, training her ears beyond Toler's cries of pain.

Soon, she heard them. They were sprinting toward her from all around. She braced herself, still running. The first arrow whizzed past her, scraping her arm. She turned in the direction from which it came. A shower of arrows was heading toward her and Toler.

Chapter Sixteen

"Toler!" Yara cried out.

Without even thinking, she threw her body over his as the arrows came flying down. He screamed out upon her impact, and immediately fell unconscious from the pain. Something within her burst upon hearing his cries. A wave of reflexive power roared out of her.

Then, everything was quiet. Yara could feel Toler breathing beneath her. She slowly raised her head up, still lying on him. His eyes were closed.

"Toler…?"

Skotad warriors gathered around her. She heard them gasping, and then shouting to each other.

"Help him! HELPPP HIM!" she screamed at them.

Two of them pulled her off of him, and another two grabbed the stretcher on each end and began to run. As they dragged her along with them, Yara saw something she couldn't understand.

There, on the patch of ground where she had lain upon Toler, was an outline of their bodies. The outline had been made with Skotad arrows. Somehow, none of the arrows could touch Toler and her. The Skotad warriors were gathered around it, pointing and looking towards her in shock. They said a word to each other, a word which they called her as if in recognition of what she was.

"What… what did they say… what are they

saying?!" she asked the Skotads pulling her.

They didn't even look at her. Before she could ask them again, she heard the Skotads carrying Toler shout towards a strange, thick shrubbery.

"Open the doors! Find Grandam! The Chief's son has been injured! Find her now!"

"What... what did you say...?" Yara stammered.

The Chief's son?!

***

Skotads rushed past her with medicine, bandages, and potions she did not recognize. They glanced towards her at times, but they were mostly focused on their critical task—saving Toler, the son of the Chief of the Skotads.

Yara shook her head as she sat on the floor outside of the room in which he was being treated. She couldn't believe he hadn't told her. She wondered why it had been so important to him to withhold that fact, especially given his propensity for incessant chatter.

She looked around. It seemed strange that there were no guards posted to watch her. She figured that, either way, she was surrounded by so many Skotad warriors, no one would be worried. Even worse, she was stuck in the mountain and didn't even know how to get out of it. She had been blindfolded at the entrance and soon lost track of the many turns in the maze of tunnels that went deep into the mountain.

When they finally removed her blindfold, she was taken aback by the beauty of all she saw around her. The walls were filled with markings that dully glistened over their stone surface. There were more markings than she had ever seen before, and many of the symbols she didn't even recognize. Sapstreams flowed along the walls, and it seemed common for Skotads to bend down and drink from them. The Sapstreams themselves sparkled, and gurgling sounds seemed to calm every passageway.

Even more striking were the Skotad women. Their long silver hair and glimmering blue eyes only enhanced their tall, slender bodies and winsome faces. Each one she passed smiled kindly at her despite their perplexed reactions and visible curiosity.

A gruff voice called out, interrupting her thoughts.

"The Chief is almost back from the search for Toler."

Yara glanced up to see an older Skotad warrior walking up to her. She pushed herself up quickly as he stretched his hand out with a wooden bowl.

"You must be famished. You should eat. He may want to speak to you after he sees his son, and that could last for a while."

The bowl contained several varieties of the highest breeds of mushrooms that Yara had ever seen. She gaped awkwardly at the warrior, unsure if she should accept.

"You are the Chief's special guest," he said, firmly placing the bowl into her hands, and then walking away.

"Tha—thank you…" she called after him.

Yara slid back down feeling out of sorts, and out of place. She reached into the Sapstream that flowed past her and drank. It tasted a little like sapjuice, but it was less woody and much more refreshing. As she nibbled on the delectable mushrooms, she wondered what the Chief would be like. She hoped he wouldn't be angry with Toler or excommunicate him for what he had done for her.

They're not Photaks, Yara… They don't do things like that… I hope…

Soon, she heard some faint voices coming through the tunnels. She could make out a strong voice among them, asking questions. The voice sounded angrier than she expected. She felt her heartstar beating a little faster. Perhaps, she wasn't as safe as she had been led to believe. Either way, it was too late to think about that now. A huge, tall, chiefly Skotad bent the corner with other Skotad warriors surrounding him, including the one who had brought her sustenance.

"So, this is the girl who had to use her body as a shield so that you all didn't shoot my son with your arrows?" he said as he walked up, looking straight into her eyes.

Yara pushed herself up quickly.

"Chief Totek," one of the warriors protested, "that's not what—"

The Chief waved him off, eyes still fixated on Yara.

"I heard your account the first time, Kaleb. Now, does this arrow-repelling, Photak-garbed girl have a name?"

"I'm... I'm Yara," she said softly, still unsure how to react.

"Well, Yara... thank you..."

The Chief reached out and gave her a small embrace with a broad, warm smile. Yara stiffened, feeling completely overwhelmed. The Chief chuckled.

"I know you Photaks aren't used to friendliness, but we consider it a custom here."

"I'm not a Photak. I'm... not sure what I am, but I know I'm not that," Yara responded.

"Oh, indeed. I'm sure you aren't, aside from your clothing. We haven't seen anyone who looks like you before... but I'm sure Grandam can help you find the answers, if you seek them."

Yara felt her heartstar pounding. It was the first time someone had ever suggested that there could be an answer. She nodded wide-eyed at the Chief. He chuckled again.

"Good. In the meantime, I'm going to speak to Toler as to why he got you caught up in his adventures."

"He's awake?"

“Yes, he is,” the Chief responded, beaming at her concern. “And, in light of the report from Grandam’s caregivers, he is going to be fine. But I should warn you... he is even more of a chatterbox than ever! You can see him soon.”

Yara smiled widely as the Chief winked at her. He walked into the room, closing the door behind him. Within a minute, there was a small commotion. The door burst open, and a stunning Skotad woman stood looking at Yara. Then, she ran and grabbed Yara, squeezing her so tightly she couldn’t breathe.

“You’re the Yara who saved my Toler!” she exclaimed. “I’m his mother, Lema. Thank you for what you’ve done! Thank you, thank you! Come! Toler wants to see you!”

Lema grabbed Yara’s hand and pulled her into the room before she could even respond. There, Toler lay on an exquisite swaddling. He smiled widely when he saw her.

"You look good!" she said, genuinely surprised at how much more energetic he seemed.

"Our centuries of Skotad research have their advantages. I heard you saved me, again," he said with a grin.

Yara smiled back shyly.

"Nothing you didn't do for me..."

"And we will hear all about that, won't we Toler? I am told you decided that going into Sunstar's rays in a Photak village was a necessary adventure?" the Chief responded, giving Toler a mock glare.

"Nothing you didn't do for Yara's Tribe mother..." Toler responded softly.

Chief Totek's confused expression vanished after a few seconds.

"She... she lived?" he whispered almost inaudibly.

Yara looked away, feeling tears coming to her eyes.

"She did... but the Photaks executed her and

her mate unjustly… all because she and her mate were kind and loving people. They took in Yara when they found her as a baby in the Greens and brought her up as their own. The same Elder you saw years ago was the one who killed them…" Toler explained softly.

"You poor dear…" said Lema as her eyes brimmed with tears.

Totek looked visibly furious.

"Well, you must stay here with us," Lema continued. "This is now your home, now and always!"

As Chief Totek nodded firmly in agreement, another voice spoke upon entry into the room.

"I wouldn't be so sure about that…" said an old Skotad woman, holding large, ancient manuscripts in her hands.

"Grandam! Why are you being so rude to our guest? She saved our son, the next Chief!" Lema said with an edge of harshness in her tone.

"She is not our guest," Grandam responded coldly. "She is the Ka-Eld. She is not supposed to be here."

Chapter Seventeen

She is the Ka-Eld…

As Yara lay in the swaddling of her new room, Grandam's words replayed over and over in her head. After she said it, there had been an awkward silence. Then, the Chief had pulled Grandam out to talk to her in private. Lema apologized over and over again, expressing bewilderment. Even Toler didn't seem to have a clue about exactly what she meant. All they knew is that the Eld were the ancestral line from which both Skotads and Photaks came. Some even believed that the Eld had created the two races. It was all subject to the interpretation of the markings.

"Either way," Toler had said, "it wouldn't make sense. The race of the Eld was completely obliterated in the Great War of the Planets many millennia ago… and they were all marked beings with clear birthlines. They were the ones who passed this knowledge down to us."

"And Grandam is a bit of a… conspiracy theorist," Lema had added.

Conspiracy or not, it was the first time anyone had ever referred to what she was with such surety. She knew she needed to find a way to talk to Grandam privately. She also wanted to get a look at the manuscripts that made her believe she was a Ka-Eld.

"What does the Ka mean?" Yara had asked Toler before she was taken to her room.

"Honestly, I've never heard that word before... and I've studied all of the markings in full detail. It may be a word that older Skotads use... I'm sorry, Yara... Grandam is getting very old now..."

Yara stared at the markings on the ceiling of her room. They were similar to the ones back in the Photak village. Symbols of Sunstar, symbols of the first people, symbols of the stories of things that had happened and things that were to come... symbols that once donned the familiar walls of her old dwelling.

There was no holding it back now. Toler was no longer in danger, and she was not on the run anymore. With no more distractions, the floodgates burst open. Her heartstar bled for the incredible Photaks who had raised her and had lost their lives for being able to love without condition. She cried for her home, her past life, and even for Kristos and his betrayal.

As the numbness began to set in, her

thoughts ran back to the words that Grandam had said.

The Eld... A Ka-Eld...

Yara's thoughts filled with questions, but her grief and exhaustion had finally caught up with her. Within moments, she drifted off.

***

"Yara..."

"Who are you... are you an Eld? A Ka-Eld?"

"I am your Guidestar..."

"Oh, you're answering now?! Well, answer this! Do you know where I came from? What am I? And why did my parents have to die? WHY?! Why did my Tribe mother have to be the one who found me in the Greens? Why was I abandoned as a baby? Who are my horrific birth parents?"

"She will lead you on the wrong path. She will lead you

on the right path. You must take both. You must take both to become."

"What... what path? Become what? Stop ignoring my questions and tell me who I am! Tell me what happened to me in the village. If you're supposed to guide me, then answer my questions! Tell me what I'm supposed to do now! Tell me how to know which is the right path and which is the wrong path!"

"They are the same path... Right will be wrong... wrong will be right..."

"What are you saying? What do you mean?! Please stop speaking like this! It's maddening! Just tell me what I need to know!"

"I already have..."

"No! You haven't! You haven't answered a single question I've asked. What am I? Who am I?!"

Yara shot up from the dream, punching the swaddling in frustration. Her so-called Guidestar had refused to answer again. Every time it spoke to her, she just had more questions and fewer answers. She closed her eyes, breathing in and exhaling deeply. She was so frustrated. Tears filled her eyes as the memories of all that had happened came back again in a rush.

"She will lead you..."

Yara jumped as the audible whisper ended with the sound of quiet knocking at her door. A note slipped under it. Yara went to the door, yanking it open and peering out. No one was there, and her tunnel was clear. She picked up the note. Its edges were tattered, and the writing was horribly scribbled. Still, Yara could make out the words, and they sent a chill up her spine:

"Meet me after the morning feast, Ka-Eld."

As she willed herself to stop shuddering, the

words of Guidestar echoed in her thoughts.

"She will lead you..."

"I guess she will..." Yara muttered to herself.

Sighing, she readied herself with the Skotad garb that had been left in the room for her.

***

As Yara followed the general direction of other Skotads gathering for the morning feast, she felt self-conscious. They all stared at her, but they had huge smiles. Then, a little boy quickly ran past, bumping into her. His other little friends all laughed when he turned to apologize, staring in shock at Yara.

"You bumped into the blue beauty!" they teased him, eventually all running off.

Yara didn't know how to react. Beauty wasn't a term she was accustomed to hearing about herself. She looked around at the friendly Skotads and winced at their strangely fascinated expressions. She was accustomed to standing out, but not like this.

As Yara entered the communal area, the room burst into excited chatter.

"It's her! The blue beauty!"

"She saved Toler. She shielded him from arrows."

"She saved him from the Photak village."

"I heard she's a warrior."

"Of course she is! Look at how strong she is!"

"Silence, everyone!" a voice boomed above them all.

Yara looked up to see the Chief. Next to him on one side sat Lema, and on the other sat a healthier-looking, grinning Toler.

"YaraStar, we have called this feast in your honor. You have done the Skotad Tribe a great kindness, saving my son, one of our strongest warriors. We will forever be in your debt. Our mountain home is now your home. Our heartstars beat in oneness for you on this day. Come join me as my guest of honor."

Yara shifted uncomfortably. She bent her head as she shyly walked up to the table of the Chief. As she sat next to Toler, the Skotads burst into celebratory applause and cries of praise to Sunstar.

Toler looked at her, completely amused by her discomfort.

"Stop smiling!" she sneered at him beneath her breath. "I'm going to make you pay for this."

Toler grinned even more.

"Oh, YaraStar… I've only just begun to find ways to say thank you," he responded in an overly sweet tone.

"Are you still in pain?" she asked.

"No, they've given me a great—OWWW!"

A few Skotads looked up upon hearing Toler's reaction to her kick beneath the table. The

Chief chuckled.

"Don't worry, YaraStar," Chief Totek said. "Your discomfort with our expressive culture isn't unusual. The Photaks who live with us also had to get used to our ways. Now, you can only tell them apart from us because they look different."

Yara, startled, glanced in the direction that the Chief indicated. There, in fellowship with the Skotads, sat a few families of Photaks. They were the happiest Photaks she had ever seen. Yara looked back to the Chief, feeling confused. She remembered what Toler had told her about taking in Light-Blinded Photaks, but this wasn't what she had imagined.

The Chief smiled kindly.

"It's going to be a process, unlearning what you were taught about us, so you can get to know the truth for yourself," Totek said. "We will be patient with you, so don't worry. Just make sure you're also patient with yourself, okay?"

Yara nodded, giving a soft smile of gratitude for his perceptiveness. She needed time to get used to all of this, and to deal with all that had happened.

The array of food was majestic to Yara. There was more sensopa than she had ever seen in her life, freely given and shared among the Tribe. She ate until she couldn't anymore, fully satisfied and energized. As she watched the children playing and dancing to the rhythms and flutes of Mira, she felt a sense of sadness.

"I wish Mila could be here…" she said softly to Toler.

"Me too…" he replied.

Yara fell silent for a few moments, and then turned to face him.

"Toler… how do I find Grandam?"

Toler turned to look at her, brows furrowed.

"Is what she said yesterday bothering you, Yara?"

"No, not really bothering. But… I guess I

am curious. I just… I just want to talk to her, and perhaps take a look at the manuscripts."

"Hmm… do you want me to come with you? I can help you with the translations."

"Actually, I'd prefer to do this alone, if that's okay with you…"

"Okay, but I will give you something that I think will help. Come with me."

As Toler and Yara stole away from the celebrations, she followed him to the tunnel of his dwelling. As they entered the living area, Yara felt moved by the airy, warm energy of the room. It was filled with many wooden shelves and a countless number of scripts. He searched through them.

"Ah. Here we go. This should help. This script explains many of the main markings that you would find in her old manuscripts. Consider it my gift of gratitude to you."

Yara unraveled it to find the meanings of so many symbols; she gasped in excitement. Then, she beamed at him and hugged him.

"Oh my, a real hug?" Toler asked, embracing her tightly. "We're rubbing off on you already, not-a-Photak!"

Yara fired a soft punch at him.

"Okay, Skotad, tell me how to find Grandam."

***

As Yara headed down a less-populated part of the labyrinth of tunnels, she passed fewer and fewer Skotads. Soon, she walked along by herself for a while. When she finally found the tunnel that was narrower than all the others, she stopped. She checked to make sure that this one had two Sapstreams flowing parallel to each other. She breathed a sigh of relief that she wasn't lost.

She walked on for a short time until she knew she was getting close. A strange smell of incense and spice filled the tunnel as she neared a large door.

She knocked gently.

"Enter!" Grandam called out.

Yara pushed the heavy door in and found herself in a room full of potions and scripts. Grandam was bent over in a corner peering closely at an old, thread-bound book. She looked up, considering Yara for a few moments.

"Ka-Eld… I see you got my message. It was wise of you to come."

"I did… because I have questions. I'd like to know… Why do you think I'm a—uh—Ka-Eld? And what is a Ka-Eld?"

Grandam looked at her intensely.

"I don't think you're a Ka-Eld. I think you're THE Ka-Eld… the lifeforce of our ancestral creators, the Eld. What I can't figure out is why you are here. You cannot be here if you do not have markings…"

"So… you're saying that all of the Eld were marked? How do you even know? Perhaps, some of them were unmarked… like me."

"Dear child… all living things upon Mira are

sacredly marked. How can an unmarked creature be alive? Such a creature would have no birthline…"

"What…? What are you trying to say?"

"You don't belong here, Ka-Eld. You don't even belong in the world of the living! You must go back to where you came from!"

"I don't even know where I came from!" Yara responded, exasperated.

"But I know someone who would…"

Yara gasped.

"Who!?"

"Someone who dwells on the other side of this mountain… on the edge of Sunstar's rays."

"But we have always been taught that everything on the other side of the mountain is dead. How could anyone survive there?" Yara questioned, eyes narrowing.

"Yes, an entire Tribe may not find enough sustenance to survive there. But one man can survive…"

"And why do you think that he will know what you clearly do not?"

Grandam beckoned Yara across to the ancient manuscripts she had in her hands the day before. They were filled with strange markings laid out in circles and spirals. Yara felt a peculiar sense of comfort seeing them.

"These are both the history and the prophecies of the Eld. They tell the history up to just before the Eld were annihilated, and they tell the prophecies of what would come thereafter. It has always been meant to guide our people, both the Skotads and the Photaks. When the Photaks decided to deepen the chasm of hate between the two Tribes, they tried to destroy the manuscripts. We did all we could to get as many of them back. Ever since, it has been passed down to generation after generation of my ancestors, and eventually to me. We have done our best to preserve and protect the knowledge within it."

"But... how can both the history and prophecies be in one script?"

"Because the Eld always saw life in a pattern... always two as one. They believed all things had duality, two powerful sides... and only when they were joined together could the deepest truth be revealed. This was how they saw all things. History and prophecy, light and darkness, right and wrong."

Yara glanced up at Grandam upon hearing those words.

Right and wrong...

This may have been what Guidestar meant.

"But... this script is in two pieces," Grandam continued, raising it to reveal a tear along the center of a spiral of symbols. "The man on the other side of the mountain has the second half. It was split to protect the knowledge within it from falling into the wrong hands."

"So... it's incomplete. What does your half

say? And how do you even know which symbols speak to history and which to prophecy?"

"All the symbols speak to history and prophecy. It simply depends on how you read it. History is read along the spiral, from the furthest point to the center. Prophecy is read from center to the furthest point. Markings have greater meaning depending on which come before and which come after."

Yara balked at Grandam, feeling even more confused and discouraged. She knew now that Toler's script might only help to identify what the symbols meant but not what they implied.

Yara sighed.

"And the man who has the other half... he can read these spirals too?"

"Better than I can, yes."

Yara looked down, shaking her head. She felt overwhelmed. She didn't know how Grandam could expect her to journey through the mountain's tunnels to the other side. Even if she did consider it, Yara didn't know how she would find him and if he would even have the answers she sought.

Grandam reached out and touched her hand.

"If you want to find out where you come from, Ka-Eld," Grandam said softly, "you will have to trust me. You will have to make the journey through the mountain. And you will have to make it alone, because if anyone knew you were going, they would stop you. Going deeper into the mountain is restricted by Skotad Law… it is considered dangerous. It is easy to get lost in the maze of tunnels. I will give you the map to get there, of course, but even I don't know how long it would take you to reach the other side, or what you would face. The only thing I know is that this journey will give you the answers you seek, Ka-Eld."

Yara stared at her silently for a little while.

"Tell me this much," Yara said slowly, "and I will consider trusting you. Why do you even think I am an Eld or Ka-Eld?"

"Because you stopped the arrows," Grandam replied matter-of-factly.

Yara shook her head, looking away. As she could tell that Yara wasn't convinced, Grandam turned to face her with an intense gaze.

Grandam smiled slyly.

"And," she continued, "because you hear a voice that speaks in a language that only you can understand."

Chapter Eighteen

As Yara walked back to her room, she felt an unusual mix of emotions. Most of all, she was astounded by the knowledge she had gained. She knew she had promised Toler that she would come to see him after her visit with Grandam, but she felt unable to face him. She knew she would not be able to explain any of what had happened. She also knew she could not tell him where she was considering going, or why she needed to do this.

Yara opened the door of her room and gasped in astonishment. Laid out all around her were beautifully woven and sewn Skotad clothes of all kinds. There was everything from warrior garbs and shoes to pretty dresses that made her wince uncomfortably. The Skotads had been hard at work to make her feel at home.

I don't deserve any of this...

She saw a little note on the top of the most glamorous dress she had ever seen. It was from Lema, welcoming her into the Skotad Tribe and offering her a place among their warriors.

Yara shook her head in awe and dropped back into the swaddling. She sighed, gazing at the markings on the ceiling. She had spent a few hours with Grandam after the old Skotad had revealed that she knew Yara's secret. Those hours had served her well. She recognized many more of the symbols now than ever before. She reached up and touched the pendant that she had whittled for her chain. Toler had been the one who first taught her that it was marking for Sunstar.

"Why am I here...?" she muttered, directing her rhetoric question to an always-silent Sunstar.

She thought about the true history of Mira that she had just been taught. Grandam's words and stories repeated over and over in her head.

"It was a different world before the Great War of the Planets stopped the turning of Mira," Grandam had said. "Our world was the home of the Eld, a much more powerful race than the Photaks or Skotads. Their markings traced back to a mystical lineage that has never been understood. They were not just the first people of Mira, they were also the only people. They were both ruthless and joyous in nature. Fierce warriors, passionate lovers. They dwelled in both light and darkness. They lived mostly in peace, but they had ancient enemies from a shadowy planet far away from here. War, however, was not of great interest to the Eld. They preferred to dwell in the depths of their thoughts and to enlighten themselves in their own consciousness. Still, they knew they needed to protect themselves. They had great planetary defenses, but they needed watchers.

"As a result, they created the Skotads, the watchers by night, and the Photaks, the watchers by day, who would also hunt and gather food for the Eld. They were not slaves, but the Skotads and Photaks were not seen as much more than the fauna that once existed in the time of the Eld.

"So, the Eld did not converse much with our kind. They thought it to be beneath them. At night, however, Skotads would at times sneak into the glowing communals of the Eld to learn at their feet. The Eld soon felt a sense of care towards the Skotad creatures. Little by little at night, they taught us about their ways.

"Hostility began to form between the Skotads and the Photaks, as the Photaks felt excluded from these night rituals. Instead of humbling themselves and seeking out the Eld by day, they became a bitter people. Soon, the Photaks viewed the Skotads not only as their competition but also as their enemies. The Photaks stopped keeping watch. They concentrated instead on attacking Skotads with light by day. Before the Eld could put the grievances between the Photaks and the Skotads to rest, the day came when Mira was attacked. Because the Photaks were so distracted by their plots against the Skotads, they didn't warn the Eld in time to ready the defenses. Half the planet was destroyed, and all of the Eld were wiped out... Mira's core was so damaged that the planet no longer rotated. This was how life as we now know it first began."

Yara had listened, feeling a sense of great sadness. As she lay in her swaddling, she wondered what Mira was like before the Great War. At the end of Grandam's sharing, and her teachings of the manuscript markings, Yara felt like she understood why the Photaks and Skotads became what they were. Still, Yara did not entirely buy Grandam's theory about her being the Ka-Eld. She was, however, convinced that she needed to strongly consider taking the journey through the mountain.

Yara took out the halved, ancient manuscript that Grandam had placed in her care. Rolled within it was the map of the mountain's tunnels.

"I entrust you with this half of our most valuable manuscript as proof of my belief in what I know you are," she had said. "You have seen the symbols for yourself… You have seen that the prophecy speaks of a powerful Eld who will return one day with a voice that guides… but what should happen if such an Eld returns is held within the second half of the manuscript. If you decide to go to find Makeba, you should leave tomorrow morning before the Skotads rise. I believe time is of the essence."

***

Yara spent the rest of the day among the Skotads and their offspring. She had decided that she wanted to appreciate all that they were, and all they had given to her. It was important to her to do this before she left the next day. She knew there was no guarantee that her journey would bring her back there.

Toler eventually found her in the communal area as she played with the Skotad children. They ran up to him excitedly when he entered, giving him hugs and asking him to play. Toler agreed, and they cheered.

Yara smiled to see how much they loved him and how much he also cared about them. He sat opposite to her, eyes blazing with concern.

"Yara, when did you get back from Grandam? And what happened when you were there?"

"I'm so sorry, Toler. I was so exhausted from all that I learned... I had returned to my room to rest after the few hours I spent there. But, guess what? I can read a few of the markings now."

She pointed to a few that lined the walls, calling them by name and explaining their meanings. Toler looked so proud of her that she found herself blushing.

"Well, I'm glad that you're okay... because I have something to tell you."

"Well... what is it?"

Toler grinned widely.

"Tomorrow afternoon... you're going to be inducted as a Skotad warrior!" he exclaimed.

"What...?" Yara responded, her mouth open.

"Yes, didn't you get my mother's note? I had told her that you would be out of your room so she could surprise you."

Yara gave him a mock glare as she embraced a Skotad toddler who had just run into her arms.

"I did... but I thought they would want to test me in some way, or... at least, I didn't think it would be so soon or so... easy? I don't know..."

"You've already proven yourself, Yara... a thousand times over. And truthfully, I would love for you to be the warrior I have by my side."

Yara blushed again. She felt a renewed sense of hope surge through her. She couldn't believe that she was being offered everything she had ever wanted since she was a little girl… to finally become a real warrior.

The thought of the mountain journey ahead flashed through her mind. She felt a sense of uncertainty. She didn't want to risk losing the opportunity to be a warrior for the Skotads. She also didn't want to lose the trust of the Skotad Tribe. Breaking their laws and leaving in secret would cause too great of a disappointment. Suddenly, the journey through the mountains didn't seem worth as much as the happiness she was being offered.

Perhaps… not having all the answers is okay… It's not like knowing is going to change anything… but it will surely destroy all that I now have…

As if in complete opposition to her thoughts, Guidestar whispered into her ear.

"She will lead you..."

Yara shifted uncomfortably as she heard it. She looked up at Toler. He returned her glance with a perplexed expression.

"Is everything okay? I hope this isn't too much pressure after everything you've already done for us..." he said with a hint of concern.

"No... it isn't. It's the kindest thing anyone has ever done for me... Your people are extraordinary, Toler. I am honored to even be here."

He reached out and squeezed her hand softly.

"Not *your* people... *our* people. You are a part of this Tribe now, Yara. Now, and always."

***

Sleep took longer to come than usual. Yara found herself tossing and turning, unable to calm her mind. The hour was nearing for her to leave if she did decide to go in search of the answers to her lifelong questions. If she stayed and gave her warrior vows to the Skotad Tribe, she would be choosing to give up those answers for her lifelong dream.

Yara looked towards the stocks and bag she had prepared while contemplating her choice. She groaned. There was no easy way to decide. Both were significant to her. She couldn't figure out if seeking truth was more crucial than respecting and giving back to the Skotads for all their kindness. Plus, the call of the warrior was all she had ever felt. She genuinely wanted to be a part of everything she had found in their mountainous haven. She wanted to finally belong.

But I am not a Skotad… Even if they accept me, will I ever truly belong here…?

Yara sighed and rose from the swaddling.

"Please forgive me, Toler…" she whispered.

Chapter Nineteen

Yara hadn't seen anyone when she took the tunnels that led to the deeper path into the mountain. As she came to the fork in the path that Grandam had mentioned, she pulled out the map. It was from this point the map began. The marks upon it indicated that she should take the tunnel to her right. After that, however, there seemed to be hundreds of twists and turns in what looked like an impossible maze. Yara, face set with determination, walked on.

The air seemed to change as she walked in. Her eyes, while accustomed to seeing easily in darkness, felt a little hazy. The tunnels were old and a little musty, but there was a scent within them that made her senses tingle. She didn't know why but something about the smell felt oddly familiar. She shook the feeling off—it was impossible for her to have been here before.

As she made her way deeper in, she was relieved to find that everything written upon the map was there with exact precision. The markings along those tunnels looked ancient and untouched. They seemed to even have hints of color in them, faded away by many millennia. Sapstreams flowed freely around her, finding their own paths from which she would at times have to jump quickly away. It seemed strange that they were mostly stable in the Skotad territory but nowhere else. The thought of the Skotads brought only one person to Yara's mind.

I hope he doesn't hate me for this...

Yara knew that by the time her note to Toler was discovered, she would be too far gone to be found. She could only hope that Toler would trust her decision. She hoped he would understand, and even if he couldn't, she hoped he would forgive her.

***

Toler wondered why Yara had missed the morning meal in the communal area. He pondered if she was nervous about her orientation although he couldn't imagine her feeling that way. She had seemed happy after he told her. He smiled when he thought about the warmth that had filled her face.

Perhaps, she just needed some time alone...

Still, as the day went on, he felt like he should carry her a meal so that she would have her strength for the afternoon's activities. He put some mushrooms and sensopa in a wooden bowl, and filled a wooden jug from the Sapstream.

As he walked towards her room, he felt a

sense of gratitude for the time he had first seen Yara. He grinned, remembering how she had tied him to the tree. Shaking his head, he knocked at her door.

"Yara, I brought you some things to eat. Your sustenance is important for today."

He heard no response. He wondered if he had missed her on her way out. He opened the door and carried in the food, setting it down on her table. His eyes fell on a note folded in half with his name on it.

Toler's heartstar skipped a beat. He grabbed it and opened it, reading quickly.

> Toler,
> I need you to know that this was the hardest decision I've ever had to make... but I needed to know the truth about what I am, about who I am, and where I came from. That truth lies on the other side of this mountain. Grandam provided me with a map to get there so that I could put together the ancient manuscript that speaks of my real purpose. A man named Makeba, who dwells on the other side of the mountain,

has the missing half. She entrusted me with the piece that she had and taught me how to read it. Please know, it was my decision to do this—she didn't force me. I've lived my entire life without any answers... and as much as it is my life's dream to become a warrior, I can't give up the opportunity to finally get the answers to even one of my many questions. I can no longer ignore who I am, or rather, who I'm not. I hope I will still get the chance to fight alongside you and the Skotad warriors, should I return. Please forgive me for leaving like this. There was no other way to prevent you from trying to stop me...

Yara

Toler's eyes widened with fear. He ran out of the room, shouting to raise the alarm.

***

As Chief Totek and Toler rushed into Grandam's quarters, she calmly continued to putter around, humming to herself.

"What have you done?! You have sent her to her death!" Toler shouted angrily.

Grandam looked up, unconcerned.

"You cannot send to death she who is not even alive."

"What?! What madness are you—"

"Grandam," Chief Totek boomed, "where exactly did you send her, and why?! You must answer for this!"

She continued to mix her potions, but eventually, Grandam looked up at the Chief.

"I have only sent her where I was meant to send her. Yara is meant to die. It was prophesied by the Eld that should she arrive, she should be sent to her death."

Grandam walked to the other side of the room. Reaching towards the back of a crooked shelf, she pulled out the second half of the ancient manuscript.

"See?" she said, pointing at the symbols upon it. "The Ka-Eld must die."

Toler's face filled with rage as the Chief held

his head in anguish.

"You told her she was on a journey to find that missing piece!" Toler shouted, outraged. "We do not treat anyone this way, no matter where they may come from!"

"Grandam," the Chief added, "the Eld passed away many millennia ago. We no longer follow these manuscripts for guidance—only for knowledge of our history."

"I have not lost my way, Chief Totek. And perhaps, nor should you," she replied coldly. "I have fulfilled my purpose by sending the Ka-Eld through the mountain. You can do whatever you want with me now, but you cannot prevent her death."

"Where did you send her?!" Toler raged. "What path did she take? What map did you give her?! I need a copy of the map, NOW! Father, we must find her before it's too late… we must!"

Grandam chuckled.

"There was only one version of the map,

young Chief. Only Yara knows where Yara is… and by the time she realizes what has been done, it will be too late!"

***

Yara began to feel disoriented as the hours dragged on. The air within the tunnels now felt a little stifling. Frustratingly, the number of forks she had taken was far more than she had anticipated. She paused, searching the map again. For the first time, she felt a pang of fear. She was sure she had kept track of her every step along the way.

But the map is starting to look so different now… Ugghhh, that's not even possible. Get it together, Yara!

She stopped, bending down by the Sapstream that flowed near her feet and drinking deeply. It tasted a bit different than the ones that flowed in the Skotad territory. She sat against the wall of the tunnel, breathing heavily as she pulled out mushrooms from her sack. She nibbled on one as she looked over the map again. She did her best to make sense of it, eventually finding where she should be.

She breathed a sigh of relief. If she was correct, then she had only a few more turns left before reaching the open area deep in the mountain. She decided she would sleep there as Grandam had suggested.

After a little while, her appetite was assuaged, and she felt refreshed. She thanked the Sapstream, running her fingers through it as it flowed away. Pushing herself up, she took to the tunnels again. She was relieved when she came to the final one that should lead her to the open area. As she walked along it, she felt surprised by how long it seemed to stretch out. After another few minutes, she paused and gazed over the map.

I don't understand… I should have gotten to the clearing by now…

The map hadn't really been drawn to scale, but for the most part, the estimations had been very accurate. She decided to journey along a bit longer before attempting to retrace her footsteps. As she did, the tunnel narrowed. Yara felt her heartstar beginning to beat even faster. Soon, she could barely walk without touching the walls.

She couldn't bring herself to check the map again. She didn't want to believe that this was the wrong path. She knew that if this wasn't the way to the clearing, she was definitely lost.

She slowed her pace as she looked up ahead. Panic slammed into her chest.

No… no… please, no…

There, in the place of the path, was a walled dead end. Boulders had crumbled all around it, and it was completely sealed off. She finally understood why the air had felt so stifling. She had been heading towards the clog of boulders all along. Somewhere along the path, she must have taken the wrong turn, and there was no way of knowing which one it was.

Yara slumped to the ground, crying out

in frustration. She was lost, and she had no way of knowing how to get back. She felt so angry with herself. She regretted leaving. She regretted listening to Grandam or even going to see her. She had managed to lose everything, all over again.

Then, a whisper filled the air.

"She will lead you on the wrong path..."

"Why didn't you just say this was the wrong path when I had a chance?!!"

Yara slammed her fists into the ground in rage. Suddenly, she heard a faint, rumbling sound. It seemed to come from a place beneath her, heading straight for the tunnel. Everything began to shake. Around her, the walls were beginning to crack, and the ground was starting to fracture.

Chapter Twenty

Before Yara could even think to react, the floor ruptured beneath her. She slipped through it, screaming in terror. She reached out for anything she could. Her hands found only falling stones and pieces of the tunnel's floor. She squeezed her eyes shut, falling for what seemed like a long time. Her body slammed against other falling rocks as they zoomed past her. Then, she heard the pieces hitting some kind of surface below. Her heartstar leapt into her throat as she cried out in terror. All she could do was brace for an unknown impact.

As Yara hit the deep waters, it knocked the breath out of her. Then, the larger pieces of the walls and the floor of the tunnel came crashing down around her. One piece hit her directly, sending her deeper beneath the surface. She tried to scramble against the force of the waters, but to no avail. She continued sinking.

Yara felt her chest bursting for air. She looked everywhere for any form of opening, swishing back and forth as she rapidly turned. There was none. As her heartstar pounded even harder, blood began oozing faster out of the parts of her body that had been gashed. She panicked, feeling herself beginning to weaken. She started clawing for anything she could find, kicking her legs as hard as she could. Nothing she did to push back up to the surface had any effect. She was still being pulled downwards.

As the pressure forced her lower and lower,

Yara's chest felt ready to explode. She felt panic-stricken, paralyzed by her fluid enemy. Desperation filled her mind. She would do anything, anything to get out of this. Somehow, that's when she knew it was the end.

Fighting to the very last moment, Yara's final thoughts were only of her Tribe mother and father.

I'm sorry… I have failed us all…

Unable to hold her breath any longer, her breaking point came. She involuntarily gasped, and the deep waters filled her nostrils, throat, and lungs. She convulsed in pain as the burn blazed through her entire being. With no moment in life more excruciating than this, Yara's death was finally an act of mercy.

***

"YaraStar… do you know who you are?"

Yara could hear Guidestar from a place far

away, but everything was black. Her eyes were closed.

"YaraStar... do you know who you are?"

It was a little closer now. Yara's eyes opened slightly. She was in a place she did not recognize... and in a form she could not see. Her memory felt vague, but she remembered taking the path to her own death.

"You should have warned me... you didn't tell me enough... you didn't tell me in time... you only told me that she would lead me... she led me on the wrong path..."

"She did... and now you are finally on the right path, YaraStar..."

"I don't understand... where am I? What is this place?"

"The greatest surrender of all is to one's own death. There are many ways to die..."

The voice was now in front of her. A small glow of light appeared. Yara stared at it, in awe of its strange beauty. Still, she felt angered by Guidestar's words.

"How is this the right path if I am dead?! And where is this? Is this where people go after death? Where did my parents go? Are they here?"

"Your mother made the ultimate sacrifice when you were born. She, too, surrendered to death. It is by her grace that you found life on Mira."

"NO! It was NOT right for her or my father to have sacrificed their lives for me!"

"They, too, shall be honored for their sacrifices... but it is not of them I speak."

Yara gasped.

"You... you know my birth mother? Who is she?! Where is she?! Why did she leave me when I was born?!"

"The greatest surrender of all is to one's own death... for the good of all, or none at all."

"I don't understand... I DON'T UNDERSTAND!!!"

"The death of all you were will be the birth of all you are. You can never become before your unbecoming. You can be powerful, YaraStar, if you choose to surrender."

"WHAT WAS THE REASON FOR MY LIFE THEN?! Just to cause everyone I have ever loved PAIN?! To cause their deaths, and then to also DIE?! And you are somehow expecting me to surrender to this? To be HAPPY about it?! A purposeless existence! Well, you know what? I AM happy! I am happy no one else will have to suffer and die because of me! So yes, I CHOOSE THIS! I SURRENDER!!!"

"Your unbecoming is your birthing. Your purpose can finally begin."

Then, the glowing light suddenly flew at Yara, crashing into her body and disappearing. All was dark again. There was nothing. It was a void.

Yara felt fear creep in. Was this where she would spend the rest of her life after death? She looked around, calling out to Guidestar. There was no answer.

Yara felt a massive surge of searing heat begin to tear at her from the inside. It built up in an exponential wave, flooding her body and burning away at her skin.

Yara screamed in agony as the glowing light burst from within her. The light blew out of her in gigantic torrents, radiating in every direction and swirling in power. It cocooned her entire body, seeming to pause.

***

Suddenly, Yara heard a great roaring. It was the most deafening sound she had ever heard. Her eyes burst open—she was back in the deep waters. The roaring filled the waters around her and rushed up and out into every branch of every tunnel. It pulsed past the Skotad territory and all within it. It burst out into the air above and to the land beneath it. It traveled through the Greens and the Photak village, over the mountains and even to the dark side of Mira. Every living thing upon Mira heard its bellowing call.

The roar… it was coming from Yara. Then, the light that emanated from her grew brighter and brighter, spiraling with pure blue light. The light traveled along the deep waters, flowing towards the ancient underwater caves. There, it whirled around, touching thousands of cocoons one by one. The cocoons were beginning to glow with many diverse colors… green, yellow, red, purple, white, and orange… all beginning to pulse and resonate with the light that was coming from within her.

The cocoons burst open in unison. From

them, thousands of people with glowing markings began to emerge. They embraced each other with joyous shouts within the deep waters. When all the cocoons were touched and opened, the light rushed back towards Yara, swirling uncontrollably. It seeped into different parts of her skin until there was none left in the deep waters.

Yara was no longer drowning. In fact, she was breathing, cocooned by a strange energy, within the waters, that seemed to filter the air she needed. She looked at the glowing people as they began to gather closer together. Each seemed to have their own cocoon.

What are they…?

Yara began to feel a strange sensation coming over her body. She looked down at her arms. Glowing blue light seemed to be rising to the surface of her skin. The light swirled as it grew brighter, forming large, bright spots all along her arms. They continued all the way down to her legs and up to her chest, traveling to her neck and then to her forehead. Her body grew in luminance, lighting up everything around her, and then reducing gently to a perceivable glow. Fueling the glow were bold, distinct markings.

Yara couldn't believe what she saw. The glowing marking... it was the symbol of Sunstar. It pulsed softly in her skin, seeming to acknowledge her as its new home. She felt an overwhelming sense of comfort that she never had before. She was not alone anymore, and somehow, she knew she never would be again.

She then became aware that the bustling of the glowing people had stopped. Her luminance had caused them all to turn, and they stood in shock, gasping to each other. Pointing. Exclaiming. Celebrating...

They rushed towards her with wide eyes. They surrounded her, their luminescent markings seeming to grow even brighter in their excitement.

A strange call echoed from some of them. They all fell silent. Within moments, they began to whisper chanting words in the ethereal language of Guidestar. Then, they all lowered their heads in unison.

"Guidestar," Yara whispered, "what is happening? What is happening to me?!"

As Guidestar answered, she felt its vibration in the glowing light markings upon her skin.

"You have awoken the Eld. You have awoken Mira... and you have finally woken, Eld-Queen... Your true purpose has finally begun."

BONUS MATERIAL FOR

THE YARASTAR TRILOGY: BOOK ONE

The Unmarked Girl

We'd love to send you a sneak peek of Yara's glowing marking, designed by Shane Bascombe & Jeanelle Frontin. To access it, go to the website below, subscribe to receive information on Book Two and this trilogy (more on this in the following pages), and follow the instructions for the exclusive reveal of Yara's marking. It's for your eyes only, okay?

www.TheEldQueen.com

#DoNotShare #NoSpoilers #OurSecret :)

P.S. If you haven't gotten your free access to the first tracks from the ***Sounds of Mira*** album yet, there you can find information on this too!

NOTE FROM THE AUTHOR

To those who have read this book:

Thank you for spending these slivers of your precious time with Yara. She's an incredible girl with a story that I hope you have felt deeply, whether through ink or light.

Her journey has only just begun. It unfolds in a way that exposes even more of her inner elements and her divine purpose for existence.

I think all of our journeys are in service of that duality. We are stripped down only so that we can see ourselves for who we are… so that we can finally understand whom we have always been meant to become.

To those in the middle of their unbecoming, I wish you the power, and grace, of surrender…

ACKNOWLEDGMENTS

Alyxander, your reaction to the earliest draft of my very first chapter was enough to fuel the fire within me to write hundreds of stories, if only to see your face light up the way it did when you found out your mother was an author. While I know you still think that this book's cover is "way too girly," I am guessing that the older you will likely think otherwise… or maybe even think other things (let me know in a few years). Thank you for being the son of my greatest dreams.

Kevin, for all of your infinitely great energy, unrelenting dedication, constructive support, and unwavering reassurance, thank you… For the authentic music we composed and produced for Mira, thank you… For the countless read overs and the pseudo-developmental-editor role you played, thank you… For every single bit of who you were, are, and will be, I thank the Divine for you… Any planet would be the luckiest in the universe to have you—I'm so glad Earth won that ballot!

To Dad, Mum, and Brian, we don't get to choose our family, but if I could, I would choose each of you a trillion times over. A large part of who I am today is because of who you have been to me. I am blessed to have been born in such a loving home. Thank you for shaping some of the best parts of me...

To my epic illustrator and animator, Izzy (Israel Silva)—the entire world needs to know about you! You seamlessly brought every single part of my imaginary Yara into the real world with a likeness that can only be explained by the presence of the pure gift that you possess. I know I was a bit of a drill sergeant with her intricate details, so thank you for your patience and commitment to this journey.

To Shane, your graphic design and artistry are equally incredible! They are overshadowed only by the extent of your genuine support as a friend for these past years. Thank you not only for helping me but also for teaching me the extra skills I needed to bring so much of this into reality.

To my friends and well-wishers, every single message, call, and comment meant so much to me, mostly because it takes a beautiful human to reach out in celebration of the happiness of others. I am humbled to know so many beautiful humans...

ABOUT THE AUTHOR

JEANELLE FRONTIN

"The one thing I'm not is one thing."

As simple as it may be, Jeanelle's adage has been a consistent reminder to her of her limitless freedom to choose "All of the above" when exploring varied passions. As a result, she has never been afraid of having a diverse lifestyle. She has been actively involved in various fields, from engineering to the creative industries. She was born in the Caribbean, in the country of Trinidad and Tobago, and she firmly believes that every human being on this planet should personally experience her native islands. She is honored to be the mother of Alyxander, the son of her greatest dreams, and she dedicates her work to him.

www.JeanelleFrontin.com
Find me @jeanellefrontin everywhere!

24578398R00197

Made in the USA
San Bernardino, CA
06 February 2019